G Damiani

Spirit and Matter

G Damiani

Spirit and Matter

ISBN/EAN: 9783337334772

Printed in Europe, USA, Canada, Australia, Japan

Cover: Foto ©Andreas Hilbeck / pixelio.de

More available books at **www.hansebooks.com**

SPIRIT AND MATTER.

A DRAMA, IN SIX ACTS.

BY

G. DAMIANI, P. M. L.,

President of the Psychological and Pneumatological Societies of Naples; Honorary Member of the First Spiritual
Union Society of San Francisco, California; of the Pennsylvania State Association of Spiritualists; of the
British National Association of Spiritualists; of the Scientific Society for Psychological Studies,
of Paris; of the Society for Spiritual Studies, of Buda-Pesth; Corresponding Member
of the Oromase Society for Spiritual Studies of the Hague, Holland; Honorary
Member of the Pneumatological-Psychological Academy of Florence,
and of other Associations for Psychological Studies.

———

BOSTON:

COLBY AND RICH, PUBLISHERS,

9 MONTGOMERY PLACE.

1880.

BRIEF BIOGRAPHICAL SKETCH

OF

SIGNOR DAMIANI.

It necessarily adds to the interest of a volume — be it drama, poetry, or philosophy — to know something of the history and social position of the author. Books, soiled and worn, perish; but their authors, as well as the truths they enunciate, live immortal.

It was during my second tour to England and the Continent that I had the good fortune to become acquainted with the author of the following drama, written in the interests of free-thought and a broad rational spiritualism. Our acquaintance speedily and naturally ripened into a friendship as mutual as persistent; and it is but the simplest act of justice that I at once publicly acknowledge the many obligations I was under to the polished scholar and writer of this drama, for such personal kindnesses rendered in Naples as accompanying me on excursions to old historic castles; to famous churches grim and gray with years; through the gloom of the catacombs; through the museum, rich in relics from Pompeii and Herculaneum, and out into the suburban districts studded with ancient Roman ruins; besides introducing me to Salvadore Brunetti, formerly professor in a Sicilian college, imprisoned by Francis II. and emancipated by the noble Garibaldi; to Baron Vincenzo

3

Caprara, imprisoned for republican sentiments at the insti-
gation of the Roman Catholic priesthood; to Count Ric-
ciardo, president of the *Anti-Concillio*, or Congress of Free-
thinkers, in Naples, Italy; and to seances frequented by
members of the royal family.

The subject of this sketch, Signor Damiani, was born of
Sicilian parents, in the ever beautiful city of Naples. His
father, a colonel in the army, and of ducal lineage, greatly
wished him and his other two sons to take the necessary
steps for becoming military men. To this end, young Damiani, at the tender age of thirteen, hopeful and intellectually
brilliant, was made to enter the Royal Guards of the King
of Naples as a cadet. Though pleased at first, he soon
tired of so much routine and mechanical drudgery. Naturally endowed with moral independence, and a strong will-
power, as well as inheriting a distaste for the brutality of
war and the war-training systems then in vogue throughout
Europe, he became after a time literally disgusted with the
miserable discipline of the army of that vain, unworthy
king, and left it at the age of nineteen, commencing at once
a commercial career with a prosperous and wealthy uncle.
In this avocation his efforts were crowned with consider-
able success.

Soon after commencing commercial business he fortunately made the acquaintance of an English woman of fine
mind and charming disposition, whom he married, and
with whom he traveled for many years on the Continent,
spending the winters in the different capitals of Europe.

Comparatively weary of travel and the excitement inci-
dent to life in continental cities, he received an offer from
a great commercial house in Naples to represent its interests in Liverpool. This position he accepted and occupied
from 1849 to 1856, thus establishing an enviable reputation
in the line of finance and commerce; but, owing to exces-
sive labors in the counting-house and the weight of ever-

increasing responsibilities, coupled with linguistic studies during spare hours, his health completely failed him, and he felt the necessity of leaving the business for rest, for recuperation, and ultimately for another field of enterprise. This he soon found in teaching the languages; for be it remembered, he had received his diploma, and had already been a professor of modern languages in his native city.

In 1868, while this gentleman was regaining his shattered health, he was unexpectedly called upon to follow the mortal remains of his companion to the silent city of the dead, — a *dear* companion with whom he had lived most happily for over a quarter of a century. This afflic-tion, in connection with memories of summer skies in Italy and the mellow autumns of those earlier years now faded and gone, took him to Naples, where for most of the time he occupied the passing hours in classical and archæological studies.

Returning to England in 1870, visiting different towns and cities where he had lectured upon Pompeii and Her-culaneum, and upon other archæological and literary sub-jects, — visiting the charming town of Clifton, where he had taught the modern languages, he selected another com-panion in life, a most estimable and intelligent woman, whom I have had the great pleasure of meeting. Mrs. Damiani, while doing honor to the social circle in which she moves, bears in her very presence that crowning grace of graces, *true womanhood.*

Signor Damiani, after a careful investigation of the merits of Spiritualism, became a believer in 1865. His religious and psychological career may be thus briefly stated : a zeal-ous Roman Catholic till the age of seventeen ; then reason-ing, doubting the infallibility of Pope, Priest, and Church, he drifted into a skeptical positivism, to there flounder for some thirty years ; but was finally brought, through the phenomena and the rational doctrines of Spiritualism, to a knowledge of angel ministry — to a belief in God and the soul's immortality.

It may interest American Spiritualists to know how Signor Damiani became a convert. I will give the gist of a few of his earlier experiences as he related them to me during several interesting conversations : —

"The thirty years of my skepticism were the most unsatisfactory years of my life. No God! no future recognition of friends! no immortality! I was endowed with a sensitive and highly spiritual organization; and therefore the universe without the soul's immortality was a failure, a farce, a sphinx stupid, speechless, and chilly. Belief in positivism gave me no real soul-comfort. It neither satisfied my head nor the affections of my heart; and yet I clung to it as preferable to the blighting theology of the creeds. Clifton, as you well know, is a most enjoyable place, noted alike for wealth, fashion, and intelligence, and, further, for its frequent social gatherings. Often I found it convenient to join these, engaging and sharing in the pleasures, the gayety, and the hospitality of the town. Returning from one of these agreeable parties on a calm, clear night in spring-time, I found myself face to face with the splendors of the heavens. engaged in meditation. Are these interstellar spaces studded with measureless stars, is the illimitable universe, is this magnificent world of ours, made to produce only a seventy-year chattering, dining, dreaming, aspiring monkey? or was it made as a school of discipline and progress for immortal man? Thus inquiring, pondering, I felt impressed to utter the following sincere prayer : 'If there be a Maker and righteous Ruler of the universe, — if there be angels in heaven as the sacred books of the ages teach, — I pray God, before these thoughts fade away, to let me know that he does exist, and that I shall survive the decay of this mortal body !' A most extraordinary feeling — strange as it may seem — thrilled my whole being. It touched as with a flame of fire my consciousness and my conscience. The conviction went like an arrow to my heart, giving convictions that God existed, and that in the near future I should have proofs of the soul's immortality.

"Two or three days succeeding this experience, while walking on the beautiful downs near the city, I met a friend, a minister of the gospel, and a man of superior intelligence, who addressed me in the following manner: 'If it be neither rude nor unwise, may I ask what are your religious opinions?'

"'I am a *Comtist*," was my prompt reply.

"'And so you do not believe in any conscious hereafter, nor in the existence of God?'

"'Not in the least.'

"'Well, who knows but that the Supreme Being, in whom you do not believe, has inspired me to question you upon this important subject? Certain I am that I can convince you of your errors.'

"'What, — you are not going to preach to me, surely.'

"'Oh, dear! no, *no!* You are past preaching to; you are a Positivist, and I shall be necessitated to give you *positive* proofs of the soul's future existence.'

"'Pray, what do you mean? You are not going to work a miracle, are you?'

"'Have you heard of Spiritualism?'

"'Oh, certainly, — table-tipping, table-turning, magic, sorcery, and all that sort of stuff.'

"'Ay, this is the way, my friend, that an ungrateful humanity has welcomed every newly-conceived truth; and yet, no truth, though laughed and scoffed at, can die out of existence. Spiritualism is a truth. It has had its scattered witnesses in all the past periods of history. The so-called dead live and communicate with their friends; and if you will accompany me in good faith, I am sure you will be compelled through evidences direct to change your opinions.'

" ' With you, my friend, I will go anywhere. When shall it be, and where?'

" ' We expect in a few days a medium from London, — Mrs. Marshall. I beg of you to accompany me to her seance, and judge for yourself.'

" ' Put me down as one of your circle. I am anxious to investigate.'

" Less than a week passed when the distinguished gentleman called for me to attend the promised seance. It was held in Clifton, on the 2d of May, 1865. The conditions were favorable, and the manifestations not only satisfactory, but really astounding."

A full report may be found in the London Dialectical Society's Reports, carefully prepared by Signor Damiani himself.

Suffice it to say, that this seance, so eminently satisfactory, only whetted this gentleman's appetite for more. The field of investigation widened. Proofs, tests, and the most convincing testimonials multiplied till they resulted in a positive conviction of the truth of Spiritualism ; and immediately upon this conviction Mr. Damiani, with a most commendable moral heroism, published the fruits of his psychic investigations and conversion to Spiritualism in three of the Bristol journals, — published them to the utter amazement and disgust of a large circle of non-believing friends and admirers. From that time to the present the subject of this biographical sketch has been a most devoted Spiritualist, introducing it to many of the higher classes in Italy and the continental capitals, as well as distributing Spiritualist literature and doing missionary work in his European travels. Many thank him for the light he was instrumental in bringing to their eyes, and the knowledge imparted relative to a future progressive existence through his own clairvoyance and the mediumistic gifts of other toilers in the Spiritual vineyard.

It was in the year 1868, if my memory serves me, that a series of letters against Spiritualism were published in the "Pall Mall Gazette," by Professor Tyndall, and the late Mr. G. H. Lewes, of London. These met the eye of Signor Damiani, who promptly replied in a most incisive and exhaustive manner; but the "Gazette" refused to publish his paper. This unfairness so aroused the righteous indignation of the author of the rejected paper that he launched forth what might be denominated a challenge pamphlet to Messrs. Tyndall and Lewes, relating to the matter of Spiritualism, and involving a thousand guineas. Here follows a portion of the text as published at the time : —

"I now offer you two challenges:

"First, I challenge you, or either of you, or any of the public who, like you, disbelieve in the genuine character of Spiritualistic phenomena, to deposit in the hands of any well-known London banker, whom you or they may name, the sum of five hundred guineas; and I pledge myself to immediately deposit in the same bank a like amount: the ownership of such sum of a thousand guineas to depend upon my proving, by evidence sufficient to establish *any* fact in history, or in a criminal or civil court of justice, —

"1. That intelligent communications, and answers to questions put, proceed from dead and inert matter in a manner inexplicable by any generally recognized law of nature.

"2. That dead and inert matter does move without the aid of any mechanical or known chemical agency, and in defiance of all the admitted laws of gravitation.

"3. That voices appertaining to no one in the flesh are heard to speak, and hold rational converse with men.

"A jury of twenty-four gentlemen, twelve to be chosen by each party (such jury to consist exclusively of members of the learned professions and literary men), to decide whether or not the facts contained in the above propositions are conclusively proved *per testes*, — *i. e.*, by witnesses of established character; a majority of the twenty-four to decide. If the verdict be that these facts have *not* been established, the thousand guineas are to belong to the party accepting this challenge: if the verdict be that these facts *are* established, the thousand guineas to be mine.

"Second. Immediately after the above wager being decided, either way, I offer a like challenge of five hundred guineas (to be met on the other side in like manner as above); the ownership of the second sum of one thousand guineas to depend upon the establishment of the facts contained in the propositions already given, *by experiments conducted in the actual presence* of the twenty-four gentlemen who have decided the previous wager. The verdict of the majority to decide in this case likewise.

" In either case, the *seances* are to be conducted in any public or private building which the jury may select, and which may be available for the purpose.

" The result of these challenges (if accepted and decided) to be advertised by the victorious party, at the expense of the defeated party, in all the London daily papers.

" I hope this is plain English.

" Awaiting a reply to this letter, and to the challenge with which it concludes, I am, gentlemen, your obedient servant,

                                                    " G. DAMIANI."

" CLIFTON, October 1, 1868."

The above is what Americans would term " clear grit." A portion of the provincial press in England treated the challenging party kindly, and urged the two *savants* to accept the challenges ; but they remained as mute, and quite as cold, too, as blocks of stone. Philosophers sometimes need to be taught lessons of humility. Conspicuous among the sympathizers and participants in the Anti-Ecumenical Council, or Congress of Free-thinkers, assembling at Naples about the middle of December, 1869, was Signor Damiani, whose knowledge of modern languages and acquaintance with many of the European *savants* gave him great prominence 'mid that Babel of tongues and friction of opinions. At this famous congress there were delegates present not only from the principal nations of Europe, but from several of the American States and from Mexico, and *all* opposed to Papal infallibility, to Protestant bigotry, and to any union of Church and State. During one of the sessions of this council, held in the theatre, San Ferdinando, the writer of this biographical paper, being called upon by President Ricciardi, gave a brief address, the substance of which Signor Damiani gave to the assemblage in Italian. May I be pardoned for reproducing in this connection some few paragraphs of the address relating directly to Spiritualism :

"ITALIANS, BROTHERS: Made, by virtue of an invitation extended by your distinguished president, a member of this Congress of Free-thinkers, and requested to participate in your deliberations, I most deeply regret my inability to address you in your native language, — a language so naturally adapted to music, to the sentiments of poetry, and the principles of philosophy.

"Freedom of conscience underlies the very foundation of the American Declaration of Independence. Our Constitution gives preference to no religious creed. Rightly interpreted, it considers man above *all* institutions, — man and his innate rights above cardinals and popes, churches and kingdoms. With the exception of a few clergymen and their willing devotees, the united voice of America is eloquent in behalf of the inalienable rights of man, — the right of each to think, to hear, to believe, and to judge for himself upon all questions, civil, political, and religious; and no priest has any business to say, 'Why believe ye thus and so?'

.   .   .   .

"The central idea, the prime thought, of cultured Americans, is free speech, free press, and free religion. The generous hearts of at least twenty million transatlantic citizens beat in full sympathy with yours to-day. As an individual — as an American citizen — I tender you the affections of a warm heart, the clasp of an open hand, and the fellowship of a soul that has sworn eternal hate to priestcraft and oppression.

.   .   .   .

"Though there are Socialists and Secularists, Rationalists and Materialists, the Spiritualists, numbering several millions, form the central column in the progressive religious movement of America. Scientists and radical Unitarians constitute the right and left wings of this army.

.   .   .   .

"Under some name, and in some form, Spiritualism, as demonstrated through phenomena, and substantiated by unimpeachable testimony, has constituted the basic foundation and been the motive force of all religions in their incipient stages. The Spiritualism of to-day, in America, England, and all enlightened countries, differs from that of eighteen hundred years since, in Judea, only in the better understanding of its philosophy, the general conception of its naturalness, and its wider dissemination through the different grades of society. It has been and is God's visible seal of love and immortality to all climes and ages.

"As a general definition of Spiritualism, the following is submitted:

"Its fundamental idea is God, the infinite spirit-presence, imminent in all things.

"Its fundamental thought is joyous communion with spirits and angels, and the practical demonstrations of the same through the instrumentality of media.

"Its fundamental purpose is to rightly generate, educate, and spiritualize all the races and nations of the earth.

"Spiritualism, considered from its philosophical side, is Rationalism; from its scientific side, Naturalism; and from its religious side, the embodiment of love to God and man, — a present inspiration and a heavenly ministry. In the year 1900 it will be the religion of the enlightened world.

"It underlies all genuine reform movements, physiological, educational, social, philanthropic, and religious; and, spanning all human interests with holy aim, it seeks to reconstruct society upon the principles of the universal brotherhood of humanity.

"Desirous of greater knowledge touching the relations of spirit with matter, men with God, and the intelligences peopling the world of spirits, Spiritualists study and reverently interrogate the laws and principles that govern phenomena and the occult forces of the universe, the histories of the past, and the experiences of the present, anxious to solve those vast psychologic problems of the ages — man's origin, capacity, duty, and final destiny."

It was during the sessions of this congress, when the very air was alive with political agitation, and with religious thoughts and theories, that this Italian Spiritualist, whose biography I but barely sketch, related to me some of the strange vicissitudes and narrowly escaped accidents of his seemingly charmed life. I recall two or three of them.

When a sportive, venturesome lad of twelve years, playing upon a flat roof without a parapet, he fell from the third story of this building, and yet received so little injury that he immediately bounded to his feet and repaired to the top of the stairs.

Again, whilst coursing in Yorkshire, England, his spirited steed stumbling, both steed and rider fell headlong down a steep hill, the horse floundering and finally rolling over him. His gayly-attired compeers and riders were startled. They supposed him either fatally wounded or dead. The suspense for the moment was terrible; but he sprung up, remounted his horse, and rode the remainder of the coursing-day as though nothing had happened.

He has also been in great peril several times through violent storms at sea, but through seemingly supernatural power he escaped shipwreck.

These remarkable preservations from fatal injuries or death, with others of a similar character occurring during a most eventful life, he ascribes to the watchful care of kindly spirits, who seem to have thrown a mystic safeguard around his life, predestining him from birth to be a pioneer in the dissemination of the heavenly truth of Spiritualism to the people of his native country. It is as true now as in Bible times, that " He giveth his angels charge over thee."

A man of something over medium height, a well-proportioned frame, a high arching forehead revealing lines of study, of scrupulous neatness of dress, a truly winning expression of countenance, a presence of courtly bearing, and a nature gifted with that social, cordial spirit so common to southern latitudes, *this* was Signor Damiani, the devoted Italian Spiritualist and the full-orbed man as I first saw him ; and time has only ennobled him in my estimation.

"Let wealth and commerce, laws and learning, die;
But leave us still such grand nobility."

J. M. PEEBLES.

HAMMONTON, ATLANTIC COUNTY,
NEW JERSEY, U. S. A.

TO THE RULERS OF NATIONS.

"If this council or this work be of men, it will come to naught:
"But if it be of God, ye cannot overthrow it; lest haply ye be found
even to fight against God."—ACTS v. 38, 39.

I DEDICATE this unadorned production of my pen to you,
O Rulers of peoples, that I may call your attention to an
almost ignored and even spurned fact, but which neverthe-
less is about to exercise the greatest influence on the destinies of mankind.

Even the most superficial observer of human affairs can
discern the deep moral disorder which permeates all the
strata of modern society, and which has always been the
harbinger of fearful social catastrophes. Wars and ru-
mors of wars; efforts for political and social revolutions;
avarice, rapines, profligacy, and crimes of blood innumera-
ble;—this is the order of the day! Yet the progress of
science, which makes us write with the thunderbolt and
travel with the rapidity of the eagle, paint with the sun
and speak with the antipodes, promised an era of peace,
order, prosperity, and morality. Whence this strange con-
trast, this jarring between premises and results? As history, that great teacher of mankind, shows how the two
most conspicuous civilizations of antiquity hastened to
their decay and ultimate ruin through the baleful influence

15

of the doctrines of Epicurus, so modern progress is coun-
teracted by the corrupting sway of a self-styled philosophy, teeming with teachings more false and pernicious
than those which destroyed the greatness of Greece and
Rome. *Positivism* — this is the name of an inane jumble
of impious doctrines, which, by reducing creation to a for-
tuitous concourse of atoms ; by defining the human intelligence and all the higher attributes of the human mind as
a simple secretion of matter, and by denying the immortality of the human soul, would fain place man on a level
with the brute creation. These are the grim maxims
taught in our universities ; and, strangest of all, the gov-
ernments, with the public money, pay and honor with the
name of *Professors* the very men who spread this deadly
poison broadcast amongst the people. Hence the unbridled
egotism, and the insatiable avidity for wealth and power ;
hence the immoral spoliations on one side, and the fretting,
threatening want on the other ; hence the most calamitous
and utopian theories, urging men to the commission of
nefarious and mad crimes, even to the assassination,
accomplished or attempted, of some of the best Rulers of
peoples. And all this in order to attain to the material
enjoyment of perishable, irresponsible self. "*Edamus et
bibamus ; post mortem nulla voluptas !*"

But the Divine Preserver of all things, as He once saved
humanity with the vivifying ray of Christianity, now, alas !
obfuscated by the dense fog of atheism ; so he has deigned
to send in our day a new revelation, which, under the name
of Spiritualism, is destined to reconduct the people, His
creation of love, to the Christ-principle. As, however, no
new gospel has been allowed to assert its dominion without a struggle, Spiritualism finds in our day strenuous opponents — marvellous to say ! — in two phalanxes at deadly
feud against each other, — the Positivists and the Doctors
of religion. From the former the obstruction is compre

hensible; but it becomes utterly inconceivable as coming from the expounders of Holy Writ, who, in the face of — nay, almost indifferent to — the invading flood of Positivism which threatens to swamp them and their churches, do not hesitate to do battle to *that* which, with *signs and wonders*, comes to confirm the truth of those *signs* and *wonders* recorded in the Gospels, and which form the very target for the sharpest arrows of ridicule of the modern disciples of Epicurus. This thoughtless and inconsistent conduct on the part of the majority of Christian ministers can only be explained by the vertigo which in our times seems to have taken possession of every order of minds.

In the midst of this conflict, great is your responsibility, O Rulers of nations! You may hasten or hinder the diffusion of the new revelation amongst the people you govern. Examine Spiritualism; you have ample means in your power to do so. If you find it a delusion, it will become your duty to stop its propagation, as should be done with every new superstition. But if you become convinced that its phenomena are genuine and its teachings godly, then bow down your head before the new messenger of the King of kings, and try with all the means in your power to confound its opponents. This new light will be a better guide for you in the government of your people; and in a spiritualized nation you will find that loyalty, peacefulness, industry, and stability, that moral advancement, in fine, without which all material progress becomes a danger for the life of nations.

Loyally and faithfully yours,

G. Damiani.

2

TO ALL SPIRITUALISTS.

DEAR FRIENDS: As I did not write this drama for you, I must be excused if you do not find in it anything for your instruction. My only object has been to spread amongst the masses the most elementary notions of our Divine Philosophy, choosing a form simple and intelligible to all.

May this apology shield me from too severe a criticism at the hands of those who, like myself, try to impart the light of that paramount truth, which we have been graced with, before so many other fellow-men.

Yours faithfully,

G. DAMIANI.

19

DRAMATIS PERSONÆ.

Grasp, a rich London Merchant.

Mrs. Grasp, his Wife.

Eleanor, their Daughter.

Dr. New.

Edward, his Son.

Patience, Head Clerk of Mr. Grasp.

Complis, Clerk in the same business.

Thomas, Servant to Mr. Grasp.

Rosaline, Eleanor's Maid.

Spratt, Errand-boy of Mr. Grasp.

James, a Young Servant of Dr. New.

Scene, London. Year 1880.

SPIRIT AND MATTER.

ACT I.

SCENE I.

GRASP'S private office in his counting-house. PATIENCE at his desk, intent upon his work. COMPLIS sitting in the middle of the office, with a newspaper in his hands. SPRATT at the office-door.

COMPLIS.

The governor is late this morning. He takes it leisurely now that he has made lots of tin; the more of which he gets, the closer he becomes, and never thinks of increasing our salaries. O money, money! thou art powerful indeed! and woe to those whom thou forsakest!—Lots of news to-day, Mr. Patience. A coal-steamer has cut in two a pleasure-boat called the "Princess Alice," and sent six or seven hundred people to the bottom of the Thames. What an exciting scene it must have been! I would have given a fiver to have seen the sight. Here are two reports: one from the Antivi—an-ti-vi-vi-section Society. An-ti-vi-vi-section! what a long word, and what can it mean? Is it a Greek word, Mr. Patience? [*To himself*] The old man is deaf. [*To* PATIENCE.] The other report is from the Society for the Prevention of Cruelty to Animals. All bosh! As if the brutes were not in the world to do what we like with them. — Now, this is too bad: the police interfering again with prize-fighting, and preventing the encounter between Golids Knocker and Sampson Smasher. The government seems determined to put down all our national sports. [*Reading on.*] Ha! this is good! another prosecution of Spiritualists! I should like to know why Parliament does not make a law to have those de-

21

luded or roguish individuals either sent to Bedlam or transported. — I say, Mr. Patience, you seem to take no interest in
the topics of the day.

PATIENCE.

I read the newspapers at home; here I attend to my duties.
I do take interest in the topics of the day, but view things in a
different light to yourself; for I am thankful I was not present
at the heart-rending scene of the foundering of the " Princess
Alice." I am opposed to the brutal custom of prize-fighting, and
I consider the torturing of animals as a sign of barbarity in a
people.

COMPLIS.

How sweetly humane!

PATIENCE.

Moreover, I would leave the Spiritualists, and all seekers after
truth, alone.

COMPLIS.

Ha, ha! You call Spiritualism truth, do you?

PATIENCE.

The Spiritualists judge it so, and their honest convictions
should be respected.

COMPLIS.

How delicately magnanimous and magnanimously liberal!
Had you sent these beautiful sentiments to the Paris Exhibition,
you would have got a prize-medal, I am sure!

PATIENCE.

You are very witty this morning, Mr. Complis; but may I
hope that you will cease interrupting me in my work?

COMPLIS.

[*Aside.*] Crabbed old dolt! I will find you another place and
put myself in yours, — see if I don't.

SPRATT.

[*Running quickly, and sotto voce to* COMPLIS.] The governor
is coming! the governor is coming!

[COMPLIS rushes to his desk, pretending to be absorbed in his work.]

SCENE II.

GRASP and the Same. GRASP entering pompously and going to
his desk. PATIENCE and COMPLIS rise, and the latter places
a pen on his ear.

PATIENCE,
COMPLIS, } Good morning, sir.

GRASP.

Good-day! good-day! [*Sits at his desk and begins to open his
letters.*] [*To himself.*] I cannot help trembling when I open
my business letters, messengers often of bankruptcies, failures,
and all manner of losses. Would that one could make his fortune without these fearful anxieties. [*To* PATIENCE.] Mr. Patience, go and see if every clerk is at his post in the counting-
house, and see that every one is doing his duty. [*Exit* PATIENCE.]
Mr. Complis, come here. [COMPLIS *approaches* GRASP'S *desk.*]
Have you had the damaged indigo placed in undamaged leather
bags?

COMPLIS.

It is done, sir; and I have made such a neat job of it that
nobody can ever suspect that the bags were not made up in
India.

GRASP.

Good! Now write to our correspondents in Spain, Portugal,
and Italy, offering them this splendid lot of five hundred seroons
of indigo, prime quality, just arrived safe and sound from Cal-
cutta.

COMPLIS.

The letters will leave by this evening's post.

GRASP.

[*Aside.*] I shall make sixty per cent. profit on this little job.
[*To* COMPLIS.] And has fifteen per cent. of colza oil been mixed
in the hundred casks of my Gallipoli oil?

COMPLIS.

Your orders have been punctually executed

GRASP.

Capital! And what price has the cargo of wheat, consigned to us from the Danube, fetched?

COMPLIS.

Fifteen shillings per bushel.

GRASP.

Write to the owners, and tell them that we have delayed the sale of their wheat in the expectation that the harvest would be bad in England this year; but that the crops having unfortunately been very abundant in every kind of grain, the prices have in consequence fallen miserably low. Say, also, that their wheat has arrived somewhat damaged by the sea, and that all we could obtain for it was eleven and sixpence per bushel. Do not forget to charge double for cartage, porterage, and all other expenses.

COMPLIS.

I shall do as usual. Let me now inform you that Mr. Patience has of late become intolerably inquisitive in the affairs of my department. Only this morning he inquired of me why we bought the damaged indigo, and what we were going to do with the colza oil; and when he saw that I evaded his questions, he turned his eyes up sanctimoniously, and uttered a deep sigh, and —

GRASP.

All right; no more of that. I will see that he will not trouble you any longer. [*Aside.*] I must send the old imbecile away, or it will be all up with my delicate transactions.

COMPLIS.

[*Aside.*] I think I have done for the old fool. His place I must and shall have.

[*Re-enter* PATIENCE.]

PATIENCE.

Every clerk is at his post, except the French correspondent, who has sent word to say he is ill in bed.

GRASP.

Let him know that so many days of his pay will be kept back as he remains absent from his duties. This is my infallible remedy for curing sick clerks. — And, in the name of goodness, have you found that blessed balance at last?

PATIENCE.

We have, sir, by sitting up, all the clerks and myself, the whole night. The difference of threepence, which caused the difficulty, arose by a mistake in the addition.

GRASP.

All the effect of negligence. I wish you would be more attentive to your duties, Mr. Patience. And what is the net profit of the year?

PATIENCE.

[*Taking a book from his desk and reading from it.*] Ninety-five thousand pounds, three shillings, and five pence.

GRASP.

What is the difference from last year?

PATIENCE.

Thirty-two thousand pounds more than the last balance.

GRASP.

Has that scoundrel of Threadbare paid his account?

PATIENCE.

He begs to be allowed a short respite.

GRASP.

Have you had him summoned?

PATIENCE.

He has always been punctual in his payments, but sickness in his family has placed him in difficulties.

GRASP.

Bosh! Have him summoned at once. Are all the other accounts in?

PATIENCE.

All, except Smallfare's, who died yesterday, leaving a widow and eight children.

GRASP.

Lose no time in sending the bailiffs to seize his goods and chattels.

PATIENCE.

[*Aside.*] What a cruel office is mine! [*Exit.*]

GRASP.

[*Opening his balance book.*] Thirty-two thousand pounds more than last year! If things go on prospering in this way, I shall soon have made the three millions of my heart, and retire from business. Had I had a less expensive wife, I might have done it long ere this. But I would marry nobility, and honors must be paid for.

SCENE III.

SPRATT and the Same. Then EDWARD NEW.

SPRATT.

Mr. New, the architect.

GRASP.

Let him in. [*Aside.*] What a nuisance!

EDWARD NEW.

Good morning, Mr. Grasp.

GRASP.

Good morning. What can I do for you?

EDWARD.

My father sends me to consult your financial oracle. He wishes to invest five hundred pounds in some foreign funds, and begs for your opinion as to the safest.

GRASP.

Five hundred pounds! Is that all your father could save in one year? I thought he was doing better than that.

EDWARD.

Oh, he is doing first-rate! But you know his generous disposition, and that much of his income is absorbed by charities.

GRASP.

My dear fellow, I fear he is too generous by half. Charity should begin at home, and he ought to think more of you and your future. Your father is a very talented man in many respects, but far from being a man of the world.

EDWARD.

Well, it depends on how we look on life. My father thinks, with Cicero, that we are here in an inn, and that our real home is that to come.

GRASP.

Oh, I see, I see! Your father's opinions have undergone a great change since he began to dabble in Spiritualism, with its table-turning and table-talking.

EDWARD.

By your definition of Spiritualism I can see clearly that you have paid no attention to the subject.

GRASP.

I pay attention to that subject! You are joking, Mr. Edward! I know how to employ my time better than that; and I prefer the steak to the smoke.

EDWARD.

It is evident that you and my father are at the antipodes on this subject.

GRASP.

It would be better for Dr. New if he did as I do. Listen: When I want a coat, I go to the tailor; for a hat, to the hatter; for a pair of boots, to the shoemaker; and when I want religion, I go to the parson.

EDWARD.

So that religion is of no more importance to you than a hat
or a pair of shoes.

GRASP.

I did not mean that. I intended to say that men who know
how to live look after their own business, leave the world as it
is, following the religion of their fathers.

EDWARD.

But if we had followed the religion of our fathers we should
now be still heathen. Religion, as everything else in this world,
is subject to the law of progression. Thousands of years ago
men began by worshipping the sun, the elements of nature,
and even plants and animals. Gradually they transferred their
homage to idols in human form, male and female, —jealous, in-
triguing, fighting gods, — until they reached the great ideal of
one Supreme Being; then came the Great Messiah and spoke to
us of the soul and its destinies. But behold a false and delirious
doctrine, usurping the name of science, trying to destroy the fruit
of the religion of love, and, by denying the immortality of the
soul, would fain turn creation into a ridiculous farce, and reduce
man to a heap of rubbish. Hence the necessity of the new revelation, which, under the name of Spiritualism, comes to destroy
the false fabric of atheism, and recalling man to the true teachings of the Nazarene.

GRASP.

Why, Mr. New, there is the making of a preacher in you! In
your place I would join Moody and Sankey!

EDWARD.

If I chose to be a preacher, I would not throw in my lot with
them; for they arouse the lower instinct of man, — fear, — whilst
Spiritualism appeals to his highest nature, — love. Let me now
correct your wrong notions regarding Spiritualism, which you
are pleased to define as *table-talking*. Know, then, that in this
very London we inhabit, a few doors perhaps from your habita-
tion, and in the presence of some of the shrewdest men of literary and scientific eminence, numerous meetings are held, at

which spirits become visible, speak audibly, and make themselves even tangible.

GRASP.

Wonderful! wonderful! [*Aside.*] This man is getting crazy! [*To* EDWARD.] But can you tell me the *cui bono* of all this?

EDWARD.

Cui bono? You seem to forget that we live in times when the man who invents a machine that will destroy the greatest number of men in the shortest possible time is called a genius, and is covered with wealth and distinctions; when to kill a man with the premeditation of the duel is called honor, and hanging a fellow-creature by the neck is called justice; in which the mowing down of a million of human lives is called glory, and to rob a people of their native soil is called conquest. Think you this the best of worlds?

GRASP.

These things are as old as man, my young friend; but how can Spiritualism mend matters?

EDWARD.

By scientifically solving the great problem of centuries, — "to be or not to be," — and by demonstrating the responsibility and final destiny of the human soul, Spiritualism will regenerate mankind. Had Spiritualism been revealed sooner to the world, history would not have registered the deeds of a Nero, a Caligula, or a Caracalla; nor would have had to record such monsters as the Booths, the Nöbilings, the Hœdels, the Moncasis, the Passannantes, the Oteros, and the Solowieffs. We already see the beneficial effects of Spiritualism upon those who in our day have adopted its principles. Alexander of Russia, and Lincoln, the abolishers of slavery, Victoria of England, and Grant, the initiators of international arbitration, William of Prussia, the founder of German unity, Victor Emanuel, Garibaldi, Mazzini, and D'Azeglio, liberators of Italy, were or are adepts to the great new philosophy.

GRASP.

How do you know these great people were or are Spiritualists?

EDWARD.

We have the proofs of the fact. Spiritualists are always sure of what they say; they have never been found at fault on that head. I myself know almost all the mediums who have sat with those high personages. I may add that Spiritualism has been embraced by some of the greatest minds of the age. Edmonds, Brougham, and Lyndhurst, the great legislators; Victor Hugo, Tennyson, Chambers, Terenzio Mamiani, luminaries of philosophy and literature, are all students of this great theme. I say, Spiritualism alone can change the wicked ways of this wicked world of unbridled egotism, of robbery and murder, of the interest at a hundred per cent., of falsifications, adulterations —

GRASP.

[*With impatience, and looking at his watch.*] By Jove, it is late, and I must attend to my business. Tell your father that there is no safety out of the three per cent. consols, and that if he wants to lose his money he must invest it in Turkish or Egyptian funds.

EDWARD.

Many thanks for your advice; and let me hope that you will change your opinion about Spiritualism.

GRASP.

If you spoke till doomsday, you would not alter my mind on the subject.

EDWARD.

Well, you will have to know all about it then. And now I leave you to your all-engrossing pursuits, wishing you good-bye.

GRASP.

Good-bye, good-bye. [*Exit* EDWARD.] Upon my word, the world is going mad with all these absurd fancies! And that maniac wanted me to become a Spiritualist! — What a nuisance, to hear talk of the other world, when one has so much to do in this!

SCENE IV.

PATIENCE and the Same.

PATIENCE.

[*Placing a roll of papers on* GRASP'S *desk.*] Here is the money which was due from Smallfare and Threadbare.

GRASP.

What, already? How have you managed to collect these two accounts in so short a time?

PATIENCE.

The money is there, and it matters little how I got it.

GRASP.

Mr. Patience, I suspect you have taken the liberty of doing again what you did a short time ago, — paying from your pocket what is due to me by my debtors. If that be the case, let me inform you that I am not accustomed to have my orders disobeyed.

PATIENCE.

Well, sir, since you wish to know, I have done to-day the same as I did before. It is a sad lot for a man of feeling to be a debt-collector; for the scenes of misery he is often obliged to witness become unbearable to him. Had you seen the distress and despair of those poor people, I will do you the justice to think that you would have condoned their small debts.

GRASP.

That will do; that will do. [*To* SPRATT.] Spratt, tell Mr. Complis to come here. [*Exit* SPRATT.] I can see clearly, that after so many years of service in this firm you are tired of your situation.

SCENE V.

COMPLIS, SPRATT, and the Same.

GRASP.

Mr. Complis, as Mr. Patience leaves my service to-day, you take henceforward his place. And let this be a warning to my dependants, that I mean to be the only master here.

PATIENCE.

Adieu, Mr. Grasp; and may that Providence which will not abandon me throw a new light on your future course. [*Exit.*]

GRASP.

Begone, impertinent old fool! [*To* COMPLIS.] Mr. Complis, you know how much trust I place in you. By your new responsible position your emoluments will be increased, with a prospect of further augmentation, as I am sure I have now the right man in the right place.

COMPLIS.

Be sure, sir, that the trust is mutual, and you may depend upon my discretion.

GRASP.

I go to the Exchange now, and shall be back in a couple of hours. [*Exit.*]

COMPLIS.

So, I am the right man in the right place! I believe you, old fellow; and I defy you to put another man in my stead! You would keep me always a clerk, would you? Very fine indeed; but I am for a partnership. There is plenty of money for two. Is there anything that Mr. Grasp can deny me? Not even the hand of his daughter! Everybody finds Miss Grasp beautiful and accomplished, but her most amiable quality, in my estimation, is her big dower!

SPRATT.

Here comes Miss Grasp.

COMPLIS.

Ha, the very opportunity! I will see what impression I can make upon her.

SCENE VI.

ELEANOR and the Same.

ELEANOR.

[*Entering with a jaunty air.*] Good morning, Mr. Complis. Where is my father?

COMPLIS.

[*Awkwardly.*] Most welcome, Miss Grasp; please to sit down. Mr. Grasp will be here in a few minutes.

ELEANOR.

I hope he will come soon, as I expect my mother shortly to fetch me in her carriage.

COMPLIS.

[*To* SPRATT.] Spratt, keep on the lookout for Mrs. Grasp's carriage, and inform us of her arrival. [*Exit* SPRATT.] [*To* MISS GRASP, *handing her a chair.*] Sit down; pray sit down. [*Taking a chair for himself and sitting by her side.*] It is so rarely that I have the honor and pleasure of beholding your lovely countenance, that I feel a great delight in finding myself in your presence.

ELEANOR.

[*Removing her chair further from* COMPLIS, *and aside.*] I do not know why I so dislike the influence of this man.

COMPLIS.

You cannot imagine, dear Miss Eleanor, the joy of my heart at this moment!

3

ELEANOR.

You are in a facetious mood to-day, Mr. Complis. I am sure you will ever be mindful of making me a partaker of that respect you owe to my father.

COMPLIS.

Respect is not the expression which represents my feelings towards you, O angelic Miss Grasp! I would do anything for a benevolent smile from you!

ELEANOR.

[*Seriously.*] I do not exactly comprehend your meaning, sir.

COMPLIS.

You mistrust your superior intelligence, my sweet lady. Do you know I am now the head manager of Mr. Grasp's business, his very right hand, and that often those to whom we confide our best interests become close family connections, and —

ELEANOR.

[*Rising quickly from her chair.*] What do I hear! Is not Mr. Patience my father's head clerk still?

COMPLIS.

He was, but has this morning been dismissed through misconduct.

ELEANOR.

He may have left my father's service, but through bad conduct it cannot be.

COMPLIS.

Yet it is so, most adorable Miss Eleanor —

SPRATT.

[*Running in quickly.*] Mrs. Grasp is waiting below for Miss Grasp.

[MISS GRASP *bows slightly to* MR. COMPLIS, *and exit, followed by* SPRATT.]

COMPLIS.

So, she feigns not to understand my advances, and bows herself out in dignified silence, as if she were better born than myself. She does not know, the simpleton, that a word of mine might demolish her father's fair name, ruin him, and destroy her grand prospects forever. But, my fine lady, I'll make you understand me before long. These presumptuous Grasps don't know with whom they are dealing, and seem not to be aware that there is the power and the stuff in me to subdue their pride; and I will do it, or my name is not Ernest Complis!

ACT II.

SCENE I.

Grasp's drawing-room. ELEANOR and ROSALINE.

ELEANOR.

Tell me, Rosaline, have you seen Edward and given him my letter?

ROSALINE.

Yes, Miss Eleanor, I have given your message; and he sends you word that he will shortly come in person to reply to your letter.

ELEANOR.

Dear Rosaline, as the time approaches for his demanding my hand, I become more and more anxious.

ROSALINE.

Why this anxiety, Miss Eleanor?

ELEANOR.

I cannot help fearing that my parents will object to this union on account of the absence of wealth in the man of my choice, and also because I strongly suspect they wish to marry me to a man of title.

ROSALINE.

How can you think that your parents would thus sacrifice their only darling daughter?

ELEANOR.

My fears have, alas, strong foundations. Those frequent visits of Lord Fitzwaugh, his marked attentions to me, and the obsequious regards of my parents towards him, make me believe that they have designed him for my hand.

ROSALINE.

What, that disagreeable nincompoop, poor as a mouse, and over head and ears in debt! Nonsense, Miss Eleanor! I have a better opinion of the judgment of Master and Mistress.

ELEANOR.

Heaven grant that you be in the right!

ROSALINE.

Stay; I hear the steps of Mr. Edward. Here he comes, and I withdraw. [*Exit.*]

SCENE II.

ELEANOR and EDWARD.

EDWARD.

Dearest Eleanor, I hope I find you well.

ELEANOR.

Thanks, my dear friend. I wish I were as well in spirit as in body.

EDWARD.

What may trouble you, dearest?

ELEANOR.

I have a strong presentiment that obstacles will arise to prevent our marriage.

EDWARD.

Have you any reason for your apprehensions?

ELEANOR.

Would that I were mistaken! But I fear my parents are wishing only for a marriage with the aristocracy.

EDWARD.

If it be so, I see a fearful storm in store for us.

ELEANOR.

To prevent which, there is but one remedy, consisting in your father hastening to ask my hand for you.

EDWARD.

How delightful that our thoughts should be in unison, like our hearts! My father, at my request, by this letter asks for an interview to-day with Mr. Grasp, in order to advance the demand of your dear hand.

ELEANOR.

When I think of it, what can be their objection to this engagement? You are honorable, clever, and industrious; the son of excellent parents, and, above all, the chosen of my heart.

EDWARD.

Love makes you partial, dearest. My only merit is in the possession of your heart. Would that I had a crown to offer you!

ELEANOR.

Your love is my crown; all else is nothing to me!

EDWARD.

And my aspirations are only for your happiness. Meanwhile let me see you more confiding and cheerful. You know what our beautiful philosophy teaches us: that even sorrows are for our ultimate good; and if our wishes be thwarted on earth, we are sure of their realization above.

ELEANOR.

True; the earthly life is but a short span, and we have eternity before us. The Infinite Wisdom would not have placed a holy desire in our hearts and forbidden its fulfilment.

EDWARD.

Well said, my dear friend; and let us leave our fate in the hands of Providence. Adieu, Eleanor.

ELEANOR.

Adieu, Edward; and may every blessing be on your head! [*Exit* EDWARD.] Would that my fears did not exceed my hopes! But I shall shortly know what is in store for me. [*Exit.*]

SCENE III.

MRS. GRASP; then THOMAS and ELEANOR.

MRS. GRASP.

Fortune favors the brave. I have played for a coronet, and I have won it. A less shrewd player would have lost the game. No fear of mesalliance now, for Eleanor will be a duchess. Poverty made me marry a commoner, and a dreadful humiliation it is! But that wealth which won my hand, wins now a great title for my daughter. After all, it is money that rules the world. Through my daughter's marriage with a duke I shall be presented at court, and the future lords, the issue of this marriage, will call me ancestress. I will now announce the good news to Eleanor. [*Rings the bell.*] [*Enter* THOMAS.] Thomas, tell Miss Grasp I wish to speak to her. [THOMAS *bows, and exit.*] O how delighted my daughter will be to hear of this brilliant engagement! [*Enter* ELEANOR.] Miss Grasp, why have I not heard your usual practice on the harp this morning?

ELEANOR.

Dear mother, I feel quite indisposed for music to-day.

MRS. GRASP.

It is not well to give way to the humor of the moment. You should try and conquer fancies.

ELEANOR.

I have not really felt able, but if you wish it, I will at once go to my harp.

MRS. GRASP.

Never mind the music now, as I have to speak to you on a subject of paramount importance. Sit down.

ELEANOR.

[*Aside.*] What can it be? I fear. [*They both sit down.*]

Mrs. Grasp.

Eleanor, you are now twenty-one years of age, — just the time for settling in life. Myself and your father have been discussing the subject for some time past. You are aware that you will possess one of the largest dowers in England, and therefore you have a right to aim high for a matrimonial alliance.

Eleanor.

Dear mother, what must I understand by a high matrimonial alliance?

Mrs. Grasp.

Why, child, high in social station! Nothing less than a lord should be thought worthy of your hand.

Eleanor.

Dear mother, marriage being the most serious step in life, I feel it my duty to speak candidly with you on the subject, and tell you that the man who aspires to my hand must first have possession of my heart.

Mrs. Grasp.

None of this giddy nonsense, Eleanor! Love lasts no longer than the honeymoon. Life is long, and we should take care not to make it barren of solid advantages for the caprice of a moment. Take my example: I, the daughter of an earl, through the want of fortune was obliged to comply with the wishes of my parents and marry a tradesman —

Eleanor.

Dear mother, your speech gives me pain. I can see no disgrace in a marriage with a merchant, for it is trade alone which has given wealth, power, and greatness to our country; and with respect to my dear father, I am sure there never breathed a kinder or better husband than he.

Mrs. Grasp.

I was coming to that when you interrupted me, Miss Grasp; and I was going to say that, although I reluctantly changed my name for that of Grasp, both on account of your father's station

in life and our marriage not being one of love, yet I found nc
reason to repent the step.

ELEANOR.

I am happy to hear you say so. You see, then, that titles do
not constitute happiness or add to it. You must also agree with
me that your step was as dangerous as it was courageous; for
had you found in the man you did not love a husband less kind
than dear father, no wealth would have made your lot an enviable one.

MRS. GRASP.

Quite so; and this only proves that marriage is but a lottery,
in which we often see unhappy those who marry for love, and
more often happy they who, like your father and me, had no
previous attachment.

ELEANOR.

But do you not think that happiness has the best chance with
love?

MRS. GRASP.

I do not think so at all. Marriage should be more a matter
of judgment than inclination; and if love does not precede, it
generally follows it. I have said enough to prove that love
should be no guide to marriage. That brings me to the point of
announcing to you the glad tidings that I and your father have
accepted an offer of marriage for you, from a suitor belonging
to one of the noblest families in the kingdom, — I mean the
most gentle and most noble Duke, Lord Loftus de Fitzwaugh,
for which offer we must all consider ourselves truly fortunate.

ELEANOR.

Dear mother, please to understand me, once for all, that I
shall never marry that man!

MRS. GRASP.

Your ungracious refusal causes me no small astonishment,
and I must inform you that it is of no avail, because your parents have in this affair decided for you. But pray, what can be
your objection to that alliance?

ELEANOR.

My heart is not in it.

MRS. GRASP.

Fiddlesticks as to your heart! Submission to our will is your duty.

ELEANOR.

I have never disobeyed you, mother; and I am willing to comply with all your wishes, except on this all-important point.

MRS. GRASP.

Eleanor, this decided and disrespectful conduct of yours makes me suspect the existence of some extraneous influence, some secret attachment, which you have not chosen to make known to us. If so, speak.

ELEANOR.

Well, I do acknowledge that I am deeply attached to, and find correspondence in, Mr. Edward New.

MRS. GRASP.

[*Rising from her chair, and* ELEANOR *doing the same.*] What do I hear? You, the descendant from a family of earls, and the richest heiress in England, condescending to cast your eye upon a man without birth, wealth, or position! Are you gone crazy?

ELEANOR.

Birth and position have no attraction for me. All I desire is to be a useful member of society. I can see no wrong in becoming the wife of an honest man, though he be without rank and wealth; but I feel I should commit a degrading and sinful act, were I to marry a man I did not love.

MRS. GRASP.

But, incautious child, are you not aware there is insanity in the family of New?

ELEANOR.

Insanity! I never heard the sanity of the News ever placed in doubt.

MRS. GRASP.

They are mad, frantic mad! Enough to say that they are all Spiritualists.

ELEANOR.

And is your objection to Spiritualism so strong that you style as insane those who turn their attention to it? In this country of a hundred religions, tolerance becomes a social necessity. Look at our own family: your mother was a Catholic, your father a Presbyterian, dear father Church of England, you a Ritualist, and I — pray do not be angry with me! — I, who have never been satisfied with orthodox teachings, have also embraced the doctrines of Spiritualism.

MRS. GRASP.

Mercy upon me! What do I hear! Abomination of abominations! You perverted child! Withdraw your thoughtless word, and say that you were joking!

ELEANOR.

Dearest mother, I deeply regret having given you so much pain; but I thought it best to make you the avowal of my new convictions. You have reminded me of the duties incumbent on my age; but you must admit that to every duty a privilege is attached. And if at twenty-one it is well to marry, and have a religion, it is also just that one should have the choice of both.

MRS. GRASP.

But, senseless child, do not you know that the Spiritualists are the most vulgar set of people? The carpenter and the fishmonger over the way belong to that foolish set. This is the society you have got into! Fie, fie, Miss Grasp!

ELEANOR.

Does not the Holy Bible tell us that in all new revelations the first become last and the last first? The Great Messiah — was he not a carpenter, and his followers but fishermen? But, dear mother, reassure yourself, for Spiritualism differs from all preceding revelations in this: that it embraces in its fold the crowned heads of the world, as well as the humblest of peasants.

Mrs. Grasp.

Enough, enough! How true, that bad company spoils good manners! The Spiritualists have corrupted you. But mark me well, Miss Grasp: you shall never marry that abominable and crazy Spiritualist, Edward New!

Eleanor.

Very well; then I will remain single all my life. But, dearest mother, let me disabuse you on one point: no one induced me to embrace Spiritualism, which was revealed to me by signs and visions of heavenly beauty.

Mrs. Grasp.

Visions? Ridiculous! They were dreams, idle dreams!

Eleanor.

They could not be, mother, because my faithful Rosaline heard and saw the same things.

Mrs. Grasp.

What! She too? Oh the wretch! This is a conspiracy! Oh me! It is too much! I cannot stand this! Oh dear, oh dear! [*She staggers, falls on an arm-chair, and faints.*]

Eleanor.

Good heavens! my mother fainting! [*Rings the bell.*] Help, Rosaline! Help!

[*Enter* Rosaline.]

Rosaline.

Mistress in a swoon! How has this happened? [*Runs to a table, takes up a scent-bottle, and applies it;* Mrs. Grasp *recovers immediately, and rises.*]

Eleanor.

My darling mother, I am so sorry!

Mrs. Grasp.

[*Walking with difficulty.*] To my apartments! to my apartments! My daughter a deluded Spiritualist! Oh, unhappy child! What will become of us!

ROSALINE.

But, after all, madam, it is not a crime. Spiritualism is not Atheism. It makes one love God and one's neighbor better.

MRS. GRASP.

Hold your tongue, you wretch! Spiritualism is a stupid and disgusting superstition. And you, prepare to quit my house immediately. [*She retires, followed by* ELEANOR *and* ROSALINE.]

ROSALINE.

[*Aside.*] Did you ever!

SCENE IV.

THOMAS.

[*Soliloquizing.*] By jingo, that was a shindy! I have heard it all — accidentally, of course, for I was passing by the door when they began the scrimmage, and how could I help stopping to hear the end? So, Miss will have nothing to do with my Lord the Duke de Fitzwaugh, happening to be desperately in love with Mr. Edward New! Good gracious! there will be a storm when Master comes to know all this, — he who is always a-dreaming of lords, dukes, and marquises for his daughter. I hope I may chance to be passing by the door when Mistress tells of it to Master. Why, it would be woful for us poor domestics, without some such recreations! I am only sorry for poor Miss Grasp, who is so nice and good. Well, I have come to the conclusion that rich folks are not happier than we poor servants, after all.

ACT III.

SCENE I.

GRASP'S private office in his counting-house. GRASP, then
SPRATT.

GRASP.

[*With a letter in his hand.*] Doctor New asking for an interview. What can his business be? Perhaps it is about the invest-
ment of his trumpery savings. What a bore! One gets scarcely
any time to attend to one's own concerns, without being troubled
with other people's affairs! Let him come, and I will give him
such a drubbing about his stupid Spiritualism as to cure him forever of taking up my precious time! I have been in good luck
to-day: four good strokes of business in two hours! The object
of my desire is fast approaching; a little more patience, and I
shall retire from business, buy a large estate, become a county
squire, and get into Parliament. I am still young, and may
enjoy these advantages for many years to come. Besides wealth,
I have every other qualification for a member. I have shown
no political color, and can adapt myself to any kind of constituency ; and though conservative to the backbone, I can solicit
the votes of a liberal, conservative, or radical constituency. This
is the way for men who know how to live. Then [*looking at himself in the glass*] I am also good-looking, and I don't think that I
should cut a bad figure as a speaker. Suppose I try. Begin-
ning at the hustings, I would say [*clears his throat, and places
himself before the glass*] : "Free and independent electors of this
ancient and noble city, — No mean thought of personal ambition, but an imperative sense of duty, impels me to come for-
ward and ask for the great honor of representing you in Parliament. [*Enter SPRATT unperceived, attitudinizing his master, and
puffing out his cheek.*] Should you confer upon me that honor,
I shall never cease to raise my voice against all existing abuses.
Through me taxation will be reduced, poverty will disappear,

and prosperity take its place. Through me you shall have new railways, new canals, new docks, new — "

SPRATT.

Doctor New.

GRASP.

[*Starting.*] Confusion! Show him in. [*Exit* SPRATT.]

SCENE II.

DR. NEW and GRASP.

DR. NEW.

Good morning, Mr. Grasp. I am delighted to see you looking the very picture of health.

GRASP.

And I admire your disinterestedness, Doctor.

DR. NEW.

You know well that interest has not been my guide in life.

GRASP.

Would that it were more so, and that you were more careful in your ways. I have something to say to you on that head.

DR. NEW.

Indeed! You excite my curiosity so, that although I have something very important to say to you, I shall be glad if you have your say first.

GRASP.

Be it so. Please to sit down. [*They sit down.*] Now listen to me attentively. You have known me from a child, and I think it my duty to tell you that you have unwittingly placed yourself in a very awkward and perilous position.

DR. NEW.

What do you mean?

GRASP.

Let me explain: You have a large practice, and are patronized by families of wealth and position. Well, I can scarcely meet any of your patients without hearing them complain that you have become a Spiritualist.

DR. NEW.

Really! And what is that to them?

GRASP.

It proves so much to them, that they will soon give you the slip, and you will be discredited and ruined.

DR. NEW.

My dear friend, I have exercised my profession with no insignificant measure of success, for nearly half a century, although I have been all that time an avowed Atheist. It would be passing strange if I were to lose my practice now, because I have attained to the knowledge of God and immortality. Should such a thing happen, I would say that the world is going crazy.

GRASP.

I dare say that when you were an Atheist you had prudence enough to hold your tongue; but now you can't meet any of your friends without at once rushing into Spiritualism and expatiating about *the wonderful phenomena, the grand philosophy,* and I know not what; and this you do to such an extent that they unanimously say you have become a perfect bore. [*Aside.*] There!

DR. NEW.

Thanks for the information, for, really, I was not aware of that.

GRASP.

It is true, Doctor. And let me warn you further. Since you have taken to this new hobby, often have I watched you at a distance, and I will not hide from you that I have discerned a strange peculiarity about your eyes, which look decidedly askance, and drawn up at the corners, Chinese-fashion. For goodness sake, take care lest the thing should assume more alarming proportions. [*Aside.*] Take that!

DR. NEW.

Mr. Grasp, with respect to symptoms of insanity, I know none more alarming than speaking of things one knows nothing about. Depend upon it, the madness you perceive in my eyes is all in my eye.

GRASP.

You take it lightly, Doctor; but I tell you that you are losing fast friends and position.

DR. NEW.

As to friends, if they are men of mind, I shall not lose them; if they be fools, the sooner they decamp the better. As to my position, I confess that Spiritualism has quite displaced me; for, whereas the other day I looked upon myself as nothing better than a talking monkey, to-day I know that I am an immortal. Have I lost in the exchange, think you?

GRASP.

But could you not believe yourself an immortal, without becoming a Spiritualist?

DR. NEW.

No; because I wanted those scientific proofs of immortality which Spiritualism alone can afford.

GRASP.

Scientific proofs! Spiritualism a science?

DR. NEW.

Yes, it has long ago taken its rank amongst the positive and inductive sciences.

GRASP.

You don't say so! How is it, then, that all the scientific men are dead against it?

DR. NEW.

You are mistaken. It is only the ignorant official clique that is against it, as they are against everything that does not pro-

4

ceed from their compressed brain. For, as the sun illumines first the hill-tops and then the hollows below, so the Gregorys, the Mapleses, the Hares, the De Morgans, the Wallaces, the Crookes, the Varleys, the Barretts, the Flammarions, the Zœllners, the Fichtes, the Frieses, the Wagners, the Buttlerows, the Trudis, the Tremeschinis, and many, many more of the same class of advanced and unprejudiced minds, have recognized the truth of Spiritualism, and classed it amongst the first of sciences and philosophies. As to those would-be *savants*, who laugh and giggle instead of investigating the stupendous and momentous phenomena of Spiritualism, if they do not quickly swallow the leek, and cry "*Mea culpa*," they, like Francis Zizzi, who refused to look at the heavens through Galileo's telescope, will be mocked by their own children and become the amusement of posterity.

GRASP.

But Spiritualism has been defined as degrading in its influence by one of the most eminent scientists in Europe — I mean the late President of the British Ass— "

DR. NEW.

Yes, I know, — Professor Tincan. Ha! he is a very funny man.* If you look hard in his face, as you assure him that he is the very perfection of a gorilla, you will see a flush of delight suffusing his countenance, and he will take you by the hand, call you a friend and a brother, and beg to introduce you to Mrs. Gorilla and the little ones; but just attempt to prove to him that he, his wife and children are heirs of immortality, and he will at once lash himself into an uncontrollable fury, and discharge an avalanche of abuse upon your devoted head. His ideal for mankind is monkeydom, void and despair. *De gustibus*, you know.

---

* The Professor alluded to, although knowing that numerous men of science, many far his superiors in scientific knowledge and mental excellence, had recognized the truth and importance of Spiritualism, did not hesitate in a public lecture to make use of the following expression: "the degrading influence of Spiritualism." Yet the ignorant multitude consider him as the very pink and tulip of courtesy and knowledge, showing the truth of the French proverb: "Amongst the blind the one-eyed man is king."

GRASP.

But he is not alone in condemning this new-fangled thing. Another scientist, not less renowned, the author of the celebrated work on Cytoblasteama, or —

DR. NEW.

I know him also. You mean Professor Protoplasterer, the propounder of universal Cataplasm. You may think him a great man; but I would rather listen to the babbling of a village beadle with a washerwoman, than to the rampant nonsense he retails to the public. For, even admitting that what he says is true, his stale, warmed-up, *Schleido-Democritian* cataplasm, as unable to heal any, even the slightest sore of mankind, does not interest me.*

GRASP.

But this vaunted Spiritualism of yours has been tested by a host of scientific men in all countries, and found to be nothing else but unconscious muscular action, unconscious cerebration, thought-reading, spectromania or hysterodemonopathy, ideomotor, chronic hypnotism, mental aberration, collective delusion, automatic action of the cerebrum, monomaniacal frenzy, knee- and foot-cracking, tendon-snapping, psychic force and od force.†

DR. NEW.

In fact a very *odd* jumble altogether!

---

* This other *luminary* of science being asked by several London *savants* to investigate the phenomena of Spiritualism, wrote back the following memorable reply: "I would rather listen to a conversation between a village parson and an old woman, than to hear Spiritualism spoken of; for, even if Spiritualism were true, it does not interest me." After this, one might well exclaim, with the Italian satirist, "O educated, educating educators!"

† These foolish definitions, and numberless others, do not proceed from the fancy of the author, but from the inexhaustible ingenuity of the official men of science, who, rather than admit the true origin of the spiritual phenomena, have preferred making themselves ridiculous forever. "I shall never give in to the spirits," was the favorite expression of a celebrated English *savant*, who is now in spirit-land, and must have given in to the spirits.

GRASP.

No joking, Doctor, with the opinion of the scientific men of the whole world! A scientific man yourself, you should know that science is infallible.

DR. NEW.

Yes, science is, but not its torturers. Judge yourself of the value of their excommunication against Spiritualism. If Spiritualism is monomaniacal frenzy, how can it be knee- and foot-cracking? And if it be involuntary muscular action, what has that to do with od force? As to unconscious cerebration, — can you conceive a man thinking without knowing it?

GRASP.

To hear you speak, the majority of the men of science are a mere set of bunglers.

DR. NEW.

They are nothing better. Science itself, in its present state, is but a sucking babe. Would that its so many nurses did not make it squeak and squall so much! Science has been defined "the knowledge of to-day to be expanded to-morrow;" but such are the blunders of its adepts that it might more correctly be styled "the mistakes of the eve to be repeated the next day." Let me give you a couple of examples of scientific infallibility: A few years ago we were told by the *savants* that the distance of the earth from the sun measured exactly ninety-six millions of miles. More recent calculations of the infallibles reduce it to only ninety millions. Now, if the men of science are unerring, both these calculations must be true; and if true, the earth is nearing the sun at so alarming a pace that in the course of a few years our planet will fall on the great luminary, and perish like a moth upon the candle.

GRASP.

That must account for the great heat of last summer, I suppose.

DR. NEW.

I like your joke, Mr. Grasp. Again: The great La Place declared the height of our atmosphere to measure twenty-seven thousand miles; later calculations reduced it to two hundred and ten miles; but, according to the most recent computations of our wiseacres, it has only forty-six miles of depth. So, if we give credence to the unerring men of science, humanity will soon be choked for want of air.

GRASP.

Good gracious! I hope this will not happen in our time!

DR. NEW.

No danger of that, my friend. We are safe both from choking and burning. I have only given you two instances of scientific infallibility, but I could go on *ad infinitum*. What do you think now of the presumption of these infallibles?

GRASP.

You must admit, however, that those men you so despise have of late made no end of discoveries.

DR. NEW.

Had they made as many new discoveries as they have hairs on their heads, they would still be on the threshold of the temple of science, for knowledge is infinite as eternity and space. Yet they feign to ignore this fact, and, because they know something more than the vulgar crowd, they pretend to decide *a priori* what is possible and what is impossible in nature.

GRASP.

To hear you speak, unless a man of science embraces Spiritualism, he is good for nothing.

DR. NEW.

We Spiritualists cherish the sincerest respect for those plodding investigators of the laws of nature, who, unable perhaps to understand things spiritual, stick to their own pursuits and do not intrude upon that wider realm of nature. They will be of some use to mankind. We only stigmatize the arrogant. selfish, short-sighted, self-styled philosophers, who at all times have tried to become a stumbling-block to the progress of mankind.

GRASP.

Doctor, are you not too severe?

DR. NEW.

If I meant to be severe towards such men, I could not find words sufficiently strong to condemn their conduct. What to think of would-be natural philosophers, who, through their unbridled selfishness, do not disdain to join in the ranks of every enemy of light, and vying with all manner of jugglers and mountebanks, endeavor to obtrude a new light, capable alone of regenerating mankind? A fig for a thousand such philosophers!

GRASP.

But what have you to say about the exposure Professors Lanky and Jackcolt made the other day of that Yankee humbug, Doctor Slade?

DR. NEW.

You relate only one side of that story. It is true Messrs. Lanky and Jackcolt, those two zealous, rising, and advertising gentlemen, succeeded in persuading his worship Pinktulip that Doctor Slade was a cheat. But numerous and exhaustive experiments made with that medium by the Nestor of science, Professor Zœllner of Berlin, proved the American to be an unrivalled sensitive and a perfectly honest man. This the German *savant* has registered in a pamphlet, which has been translated in every language, and in which the character of Dr. Slade has been fully vindicated. Let us be fair, my friend; let us be fair.

GRASP.

But, Dr. New, you would tyrannically impose the belief of Spiritualism to every one.

DR. NEW.

Spiritualism is not a matter of belief, but of knowledge; and we never intended to force that knowledge upon any one. It is the self-styled men of science who unsolicited keep bawling out, "*Non credo!*" until we Spiritualists have become skeptical of their unbelief.

GRASP.

You seem to have taken up the shining sword of Achilles in defence of Spiritualism. Let me remind you, however, that of late we have had a host of other pretentious and regenerating *isms*, which have proved anything but beneficial to the world, — Socialism, Internationalism, Communism, Nihilism, and Revolutionism. You will therefore excuse me if I doubt the efficacy for good of this new *ism*.

DR. NEW.

The *isms* you deplore are the offspring of other dire *isms*, — Positivism, Utilitarianism, Egotism, Materialism, and Atheism, all springing from the same stock of mother Ignorance. Spiritualism, by dispelling the dark cloud of ignorance, will abolish war, with its costly standing armies, and with them poverty, crime, the prison, and the scaffold. These will be some of the effects of the spreading of this new light, which is recognized " by those who see " as the greatest event of our century.

GRASP.

Doctor, Demosthenes never spoke better than you; but I will tell you that all your eloquence will never make a Spiritualist of me. I have done my duty in warning you of the ruinous tendency of Spiritualism, and now I wash my hands clean of the matter.

DR. NEW.

I am much obliged for your kind intentions, and assure you in return that you can no more wean me from Spiritualism than you could from mathématics. And now, Mr. Grasp, we will enter into another subject of very great importance to us both. You know the deep affection and regard which my family has always cherished for that dear child of yours. This affection, this special regard for your daughter, has been shared in the highest degree by my son Edward; and I come here to-day, in his name and mine, to ask for the great privilege of her hand for him.

GRASP.

[*Rising quickly from his chair.*] Dr. New, methinks you are joking! And if you are not, let me tell you that you have made a grievous miscalculation!

Dr. New.

[*Rising also.*] Mr. Grasp, I have been doing neither thing. Pray, what can be your objection to this marriage?

Grasp.

[*Rather warmly.*] Sir, you forget that my daughter will possess one of the largest fortunes in England, and that your son has neither means nor position.

Dr. New.

You are mistaken in both points. I have saved enough to provide for my son, that he may live as a gentleman. As to his position, if I asked you who he was that built St. Paul's, the name of Wren would at once come upon your lips; but if I requested the name of the richest merchant in London a hundred years ago, you could not tell me. This is the difference between an architect and a millionnaire. The one leaves the impress of his genius for the admiration of posterity; the other, unless he be a Peabody, disappears, with his wealth and his pride, from the memory of men.

Grasp.

Doctor, to cut short this useless interview, let me tell you that I refuse your son's offer, insomuch that my daughter is already designed for a nobleman of the highest rank.

Dr. New.

But have you consulted your daughter's inclinations?

Grasp.

I have not, because I needed it not.

Dr. New.

And if your daughter loved my son, and would not have your nobleman?

Grasp.

I do not believe in either hypothesis; but were it so, I would not alter my resolution.

Dr. New.

But if, through that forced union, your child were to pine away and die of grief?

Grasp.

Then she would die a duchess, and her tomb would be adorned with the most splendid blazon of nobility in the kingdom.

Dr. New.

Merchant Grasp, I have always suspected you of avarice and ambition, but I never thought you capable of becoming the dishonorer and murderer of your own offspring. Adieu, Mr. Grasp. And may the Eternal Infinite illumine your mind and touch your heart. [*Exit.*]

Grasp.

The impertinent old beggar! Aspiring to the hand of my daughter, who is sought after by the greatest nobility of the realm! And insinuating, too, that she could so demean herself as to fall in love with that starveling of his son! But my name is not Benjamin Grasp, if within a month my daughter has not become Lady Loftus de Fitzwaugh!

ACT IV.

SCENE I.

GRASP'S drawing-room.

GRASP.

[*Pacing the room excitedly.*] The more I think of it the more I am enraged at the incredible audacity of those plebeians! My daughter, one of the richest heiresses in Europe, and the grand-daughter of an earl, becoming the wife of a poverty-stricken, trumpery architect! But can it be that Eleanor has so forgotten herself as to listen to the advances of that snob? Impossible! No, not impossible, — only improbable; for who can fathom the heart and mind of woman? Anyhow, I will soon solve the question!

SCENE II.

MRS. GRASP and the Same.

MRS. GRASP.

[*Much excited.*] Oh, Grasp, Grasp! You are there at last! Behold the most unhappy, the most miserable of women! Your daughter! — your unhappy, ill-fated daughter!

GRASP.

Calm yourself, calm yourself. I suspect what vexes you. Can it be that Eleanor has really fallen in love with that presumptuous ragamuffin?

MRS. GRASP.

True? Alas, too true! But your cool and calm demeanor shows clearly that you do not know the extent of our misfortune.

GRASP.

Good gracious! What has happened, then? Speak!

MRS. GRASP.

And that wretch, Rosaline, in the conspiracy! Well, then, know that your daughter, your hapless daughter, is — ah me! [*Falls on an arm-chair in a fainting fit.*]

GRASP.

Good heavens! What can have happened? [*Rings the bell.*]

———

SCENE III.

ROSALINE and the Same.

ROSALINE.

What! Mistress in a swoon again? Don't be afraid, sir; she will soon recover.

GRASP.

Speak, you miserable wretch! What has happened to my daughter?

ROSALINE.

[*Having already applied the usual scent-bottle.*] Don't be in such a flutter, sir! Miss Grasp is in her room, safe and sound.

GRASP.

For goodness sake, then, what is all this about?

MRS. GRASP.

[*With a twitch of one side of her body, and faintly.*] Deluge—

GRASP.

The deluge?

MRS. GRASP.

A spur—

GRASP.

My daughter becoming a spur?

MRS. GRASP.

[*Twitching the other side of her person.*] A spit—

GRASP.

A spit?

MRS. GRASP.

[*Rising from her chair with uplifted arms, and with a stentorian, convulsive voice.*] A de-lu-ded spir-it-ualist! [*Falls again insensible on the arm-chair.*]

GRASP.

Ah! I breathe freely! Rosaline, is there any truth in this?

ROSALINE.

[*Busy bathing the temples of* MRS. GRASP *with eau de Cologne.*] Quite true, sir; and she has been much happier ever since.

MRS. GRASP.

[*Regaining her senses, and rising again.*] You abominable woman! Out of my house at once!

ROSALINE.

Pay me a month's wages, and I will go at once.

GRASP.

Don't be in such a hurry, Mrs. Grasp. She must remain, for I mean to sift this matter to the bottom. Meanwhile calm yourself. The evil is not so great that it cannot be repaired. Our daughter is but a child, and we will bring her to her senses. You are in want of rest; return to your room, and after I have examined into this affair, we will speak to our silly, misled child. [*To* ROSALINE.] Rosaline, after attending to Mrs. Grasp return here with Thomas.

MRS. GRASP.

Ah! poor me! Oh dear, oh dear! [*Exit,* ROSALINE *following her.*]

GRASP.

Botheration! Who would have thought of the falling of this thunderbolt? My daughter in love with a beggar, and perverted by this abominable Spiritualism! But see if I don't clear her brains of all this nonsense! [*Rings the bell.*]

SCENE IV.

The Same; THOMAS and ROSALINE.

GRASP.

Listen to me well: I command that all letters to and from Miss Grasp be brought into my hands immediately. Do you understand?

THOMAS,
ROSALINE. } All right, sir. [*Exit* GRASP.]

THOMAS.

What a hubbub in this house, to be sure!—and all on account of that horrible Lord Fitzwaugh! He had better be called Lord Fitz-owe, since he is over head and ears in debt.

ROSALINE.

I would rather call him Fitz-woe, on account of the misery he has brought into this house. What a nice husband to propose for that good, dear young lady!—a hop-pole, red-haired, and a parrot's nose. And how nice he talks!—"Thweet Mith Gwathp, waugh-waugh, I hope to thee you thalubriouth."

THOMAS.

Upon my word, Rosaline, I never saw a better photograph of mi-lord than that. Do you know, I happened to be near the door when Mistress fainted twice? It was quite tragic. But I could not understand what she meant when she made such a fuss about Spiritualism. What is that Spiritualism?

ROSALINE.

Never mind that, Thomas. If I would try to explain what is
meant by Spiritualism, most likely you would neither believe
me nor understand it.

THOMAS.

Come, come! Am I such a fool that I cannot understand what
you can?

ROSALINE.

Well, then, Spiritualism means seeing and talking with the
so-called dead, who are more alive than we.

THOMAS.

And is that all? And is it for this that Master and Mistress
make such a hullabaloo? Why, my mother and my sisters have
over and over again told me that they have both seen and talked
with spirits; besides, when I visit them I hear myself mysterious knocks, which could not be produced by any one in the
house; and my family ain't people for telling fibs and practical
joking.

ROSALINE.

Thomas, I am so glad you know so much about Spiritualism,
because I can tell you now that I often see and talk with my
dear, dear mother.

THOMAS.

All this is quite natural. We all know we have an immortal
soul; and why should not those who have gone before us be able
to manifest and tell us of their undiminished love?

ROSALINE.

Just so. Yet there are men who call themselves philosophers
and won't believe a word of it. Before I came to this house I
was living at a Mr. Faraday's, who styled himself a natural
philosopher. It was the time of table-turning, you know; and
although everybody admitted that the table did turn, my master
alone was obstinate in saying it didn't. And what must he
do? He must go to a great expense in having a curious sort of
table made, defying the spirits to move it.

THOMAS.

And what was the upshot?

ROSALINE.

Well, one evening he invited lots of his friends, all doctors, professors, and philosophers, and made them sit round this queer article of furniture. Jane, the cook, and I, who were all curiosity, placed ourselves behind the door. At first all was silence; then we heard Master shout, "Spirits, move this table if you can!" when, law! Thomas, the table began with spinning round and round, and then rising in the air, went and bumped against the ceiling.* You may imagine the long faces of the wiseacres present, who broke up in disgust. From that time Master used to go into a rage if anybody attempted to touch on the subject of table-turning.†

THOMAS.

What a farce!

ROSALINE.

But that's not all. When Jane and I went down into the kitchen we just put our hands lightly on the heavy table there, and in a moment it went round like a spindle. From that time I lost all good opinion of those blockheads of philosophers.

THOMAS.

And serve them right, I say. I'll tell you what I have been thinking: if I were Miss Grasp, I would give the slip to mi-lord Fitzwaugh, and elope with Mr. Edward New.

ROSALINE.

No, Thomas, that would never do; because in the Spiritual books which Miss Eleanor gives me to read it is said that we must restrain our passions, and avoid giving pain to others.

---

* This is literally historical.

† This is also historical, as is proved by the never-to-be-forgotten, illogical and savage letter which the Professor in 1861 wrote to Sir Emerson Tennent, who hazarded to invite him to assist at a séance with Mr. Home.

THOMAS.

Dear Rosaline, these are very good sentiments, and you could bring me to think in the same way. Tell me, dear, don't you believe that if we were joined in wedlock we should make a very happy couple? Will you consent to my wooing you?

ROSALINE.

Dear Thomas, since I find you do not scoff at these serious things, I will confess that I have been long attached to you.

THOMAS.

Give me your hand, then, and say we are engaged.

ROSALINE.

Here it is; and may God bless our engagement! [*A bell is heard.*] Oh, this is Miss Eleanor's bell, and I must go. Good-bye, Thomas.

THOMAS.

God bless you, Rosaline!

[*Exit both at opposite sides of the stage.*]

SCENE V.

GRASP and MRS. GRASP entering together.

GRASP.

I am glad to see you somewhat calmer. This is the frame of mind best adapted to meet difficulties. A great misfortune has befallen us; but accidents will happen in the best regulated families. We will call our daughter, and see if we cannot persuade her to forget that beggar and the follies of Spiritualism, and induce her to accept the nobleman of our choice. You know she has ever been good and obedient, and I am sure she will not thwart us in our desire.

Mrs. Grasp.

It is clear that you do not know your daughter's character. I have exhausted every argument to induce her to forget that fellow, and that vulgar and absurd Spiritualism, and to persuade her to do our bidding; but all to no purpose. You should have seen the set determination with which she declared her unwillingness to enter into our views. I think yours will be all time lost.

Grasp.

Do not say so. She is a mere child, and at her age women change like a weathercock. You cannot forget that when I asked you in marriage your heart was set upon Captain Bolt; yet you were soon talked into persuasion, and married me instead.

Mrs. Grasp.

Yes; but I have ever been strong-minded, whilst your daughter is incapable of restraining her feelings, and is as weak as water.

Grasp.

According to your own account, her behavior seems to betray anything but weakness. Anyhow, we will talk to her, and see if we cannot conquer her obstinacy. [*Rings the bell.*]

SCENE VI.

Thomas and the Same.

Grasp.

Thomas, tell Miss Grasp that I want to speak to her. [Thomas *bows, and exit.*] And pray, Mrs. Grasp, keep your temper, and do not interrupt me.

Mrs. Grasp.

I wish you good luck.

5

SCENE VII.

ELEANOR and the Same.

ELEANOR.

Dear father and mother, I come at your bidding; but if the object of calling me into your presence is to induce me to betray the most sacred feelings of my heart, I think it right at once to declare that I cannot do so.

MRS. GRASP.

[*Aside.*] The weak, deluded girl!

GRASP.

[*Aside.*] Weak? Very! [*To* ELEANOR.] Miss Grasp, we have not called you here to know your mind, but for you to learn ours. Recollect the duties of children towards their parents.

ELEANOR.

I never neglected those duties, and I now declare my readiness to comply with all your wishes except giving my hand to a man I do not love.

GRASP.

Stuff and nonsense! You must listen to reason. And to begin with: Let me hear from your own lips that there is no truth in your having so demeaned yourself as to encourage the advances of that beggarly fellow, Edward New. Say that I have been grievously misinformed on that point.

ELEANOR.

Dear father, I have formed a strong attachment to Edward New, whom I know to be both good and honorable. He is not rich: but where is the mortal on whom fortune lavishes every gift?

GRASP.

What! you, the best educated girl in England, and the heiress of a princely fortune, cast your eye upon a man without wealth, title, or position! And could you for a moment think that we should sanction such a degradation?

ELEANOR.

I can see no degradation in loving a just and worthy man; and I feel that I can never love any other than him.

GRASP.

Very romantic, this! But I will tell you that you will have to forget him, for I have already accepted for you the offer of a nobleman of high standing; and as my word has been given, him you shall marry.

ELEANOR.

For the respect I owe to myself, I shall never consent to do that.

MRS. GRASP.

Oh, unhappy child! Is this the way to reward us for all the care and attention we have bestowed upon you?

GRASP.

Shame, shame, for your disobedience, and for engaging yourself without consulting your parents! By your obstinacy you expose your father to the obloquy of having failed in his word to a nobleman of the highest rank.

ELEANOR.

It never entered my mind to disobey or displease my parents. I have not engaged my hand, but I have become attached to Edward New, whom I have known as a child. If I have given you pain, I sincerely beg your pardon. As to exposing you to the unpleasantness of a refusal, — excuse me, dear father, but before deciding of my destiny you might at least have consulted me. Throw upon me all the responsibility of that refusal. May I now be allowed to retire?

GRASP.

Not yet, Miss Grasp, as I have another account to settle with you. Tell me, can it be possible that you have also been perverted into the supremely stupid superstition of spirit-rapping?

ELEANOR.

With a devout and thankful heart I have received the heavenly revelation of Spiritualism; and it is in virtue of my new convictions if, to avoid giving you pain, I am ready to renounce to the man of my affections.

GRASP.

And give your hand to the nobleman of our choice?

ELEANOR.

That I shall never do, to avert shame worse than death from me and remorse to you in your old age.

GRASP.

Enough, enough! Prepare to leave to-day with your mother for our country seat, there to remain until you have become wiser!

ELEANOR.

I shall obey.   [*Exit.*]

MRS. GRASP.

I told you, Mr. Grasp, that speaking to our daughter would be useless. Those low tastes of our child show that she has not inherited the noble blood of my family, the Earls of Grandton.

GRASP.

She may not have inherited the blood of the Grandtons, but she has decidedly taken yours, for she is as obstinate as yourself. Besides, it is you who have educated her, whom I have scarcely ever seen.

MRS. GRASP.

Indeed! Had I been obstinate, I should not have married you, Mr. Grasp, for you know I never loved you!

GRASP.

And you cannot ignore that I only married you for your connection, and did not care a button for you. So, you see, there has been no love lost between us!

Mrs. Grasp.

Your speech does not testify favorably for your taste, sir; and I see too late the consequences for a woman of noble blood marrying a tradesman!

Grasp.

And I the folly of connecting myself with a family of beggars, who come to devour my good dinners, and then think themselves too great to receive me into their society!

Mrs. Grasp.

No more of this, Mr. Grasp! I rejoice in the idea of leaving for the country!—anywhere better than in your presence, sir! Good-bye!

Grasp.

I wish you a good journey, my noble spouse, and, pray, don't be in a hurry to come back!

Mrs. Grasp.

You uncouth bear! [*Exit.*]

Grasp.

For a wonder, she hasn't fainted again! I begin to think that life is not a bed of roses, after all. Marriage, which I thought would advance me in station, has proved a costly disappointment. Instead of a son to inherit my princely fortune, and maintain the honor of my name, I am doomed to bestow it upon a daughter with a mind so perverted as to join her mother in thwarting and insulting me. But riches are left me still; and if I cannot find happiness at home, I shall seek it in the honors of public life, when I retire from business, and see the gates of St. James's open for me.

SCENE VIII.

THOMAS and the Same.

THOMAS.

[*With letters on a silver tray.*] Please, sir, these letters have just arrived. [*Exit.*]

GRASP.

[*Examining the letters.*] They are all for my wife and daughter. — This is for Mrs. Grasp. I will open it, for I must know henceforward what is going on in this house. [*Opens the letter.*] A bill from that witch perfumer, Madam Rachel. [*Reading aloud.*] "Enamelling pearl paste, to make beautiful forever, three hundred guineas." The deuce! "Balsam of Arcadia, and Oriental skin-emollient, twelve bottles, one hundred and twenty guineas." Bagatelle! "Elixir of youth, six bottles, sixty guineas." Very cheap! "Ambrosian scent, twelve bottles, twelve guineas." She must have stolen it! "*Nota bene:* Madam Rachel respectfully informs Mrs. Grasp, that as the above is a long-standing account, if cash is not received within twenty-four hours, Madam Rachel will be compelled to dispose of Mrs. Grasp's diamond bracelet." Ha, ha! capital! My better half was unwise to tell me she would pawn her jewels if I did not give her money for these hare-brained extravagances; for I quietly had the diamonds replaced by paste so natural as to have deceived even Madam Rachel! It is well that the law cannot compel me to pay in this case. [*Opens another letter.*] This is for Miss Grasp. "May good angels reward you for your generous contribution for the defence of persecuted mediums!" Confound them all! I should like to see them at the bottom of the sea! [*Crumples up the letter, and opens another.*] This is also for my daughter. [*Reads.*] "Received with thanks from Miss Grasp the sum of ten pounds in aid of the Society for the Protection of Animals liable to Vivisection." Very fine, this! Protecting the brutes, and skinning me alive! I must put a stop to all this foolery, or I shall be ruined! [*Takes up another letter.*] Also for Miss Grasp. What an elegant, perfumed envelope!

From whom can it be? [*Opens the letter and reads.*] "Angelic Miss Grasp!" [*Turns the sheet to look at the signature.*] Thunder and lightning! A love-letter to my daughter from that cur, Complis!

SCENE IX.

COMPLIS and the Same

COMPLIS.

[*In a drawling tone.*] Good-morning, sir. I hope I see you well.

GRASP.

Mr. Complis, I have no further need of your services; you may find another situation.

COMPLIS.

[*Sarcastically.*] You don't mean it? And why, pray?

GRASP.

I refuse to give you any reason. You may retire. [*Goes to ring the bell.*]

COMPLIS.

Stop, stop, Mr. Grasp. Don't be in such a hurry. My name is not Patience. A civil question requires a civil answer. Again I request to know your reason for discharging me.

GRASP.

[*Showing him his letter.*]. That is the reason, you presumptuous puppy!

COMPLIS.

[*Coolly.*] And why presumptuous? Except the coin, am I not better than you? I am the son of a barrister, and you of a pedlar, who, like yourself, made his fortune by forgeries and robberies.

GRASP.

Hush, hush, miserable wretch! Recollect that I have you in my power!

COMPLIS.

Or rather that you are in mine, as one word from me and you
will be done for.

GRASP.

Be careful, fellow, for I can have you transported!

COMPLIS.

I like that! Perhaps you don't know that the rope that would
hang me would choke you also. That compromising document
which I told you I destroyed is still in my possession, and I may
turn Queen's evidence!

GRASP.

Hush! don't speak so loud! Where is that document?

COMPLIS.

The document is scrupulously preserved where a liberal consideration may find it.

GRASP.

How much for that paper?

COMPLIS.

[*Opening his hand and showing it to* GRASP.] Five thousand
pounds, and cheap at the price.

GRASP.

None of this nonsense! The paper is not worth that. I'll
give you two thousand.

COMPLIS.

Five, or I keep the document.

GRASP.

I will give you three thousand, and see you hanged before I
give you another penny.

COMPLIS.

Well, I'll be generous. It is a bargain.

GRASP.

Be here to-night at eleven o'clock with the document, and you will find the money ready.

COMPLIS.

I shall not fail to render you that little service, Grasp. [*Going.*] Don't, don't come to the door. [*Exit.*]

GRASP.

The infamous and treacherous scoundrel! He has caught me! But even without that document he knows enough of my affairs to destroy me! Could I not—ha, money is power!—could I not make that wretch disappear? His lodgings are near the Thames embankment, and he will have to leave them at about ten to-night. For extreme evils extreme remedies, and diamond cut diamond. [*Goes to his desk and writes.*] [*To himself as he goes on writing.*] "Mr. Sharkey, as soon as you receive this, start for my office, and wait there for me until I come. Bring with you your friend Bill Loom, if you can." [*Rings the bell.*]

SCENE X.

THOMAS and the Same.

GRASP.

Thomas, go at once to No. 950 Narrow Thames Street, and deliver this note to the person who lives there. As it is far, take a cab; lose no time.

THOMAS.

It shall be done, sir. [*To himself.*] A very queer address, this. [*Exit.*]

GRASP.

Complis, you would have your little game with me, but you did not know that I could play the knave as well as you!

ACT V.

SCENE I.

Library in Dr. New's house.

EDWARD NEW.

My father is late in returning. Had he good tidings for me, he would not have delayed so long. Alas, I fear a refusal! But I am prepared for the worst, and the blow will find me resigned, as befits one who knows that all is ordained for our ultimate good.

SCENE II.

Dr. New, the Same, and eventually James.

EDWARD.

Dear father, I can read in your countenance the confirmation of my fears.

DR. NEW.

Edward, my dear boy, it is all over. Mr. Grasp has not only refused your offer, but has taken the opportunity of insulting us by qualifying your proposal as presumptuous. Moreover he avers that his daughter is already promised to a nobleman. I feel deeply for you, but I am sure that you will stand this trial as behooves an adept to our sublime philosophy.

EDWARD.

You are right. My grief is intense, but you see me resigned.

DR. NEW.

Well done, Edward. The strokes of fortune are intended to strengthen the soul, and the severity of this will fully prepare you for those trials with which your coming days are sure to be strewed.

EDWARD.

What troubles me most is the thought of the sufferings of that bright angel, who, besides the pain of our separation, will have to endure the importunities of her parents in trying to force her into an abhorred union.

DR. NEW.

I fully appreciate your feelings; but Eleanor is endowed with a sterling heart, and I am sure she will endure her grief with fortitude.

EDWARD.

I do not doubt that. Would that this consideration could in any degree console me!

DR. NEW.

I can understand that her strength of mind and powers of resignation are but poor consolation to you. Happily, she, like you, knows that sorrow is the crucible where the soul gets refined.

[*Enter* JAMES.]

JAMES.

Please, sir, a servant has called, desiring you to visit his sick mistress immediately.

DR. NEW.

I come. [*Exit* JAMES.] I am sorry to leave you at this moment. Look upwards, Edward; look upwards.

EDWARD.

Good-bye, father. May God reward you for your great kindness and sympathy.

DR. NEW.

Adieu, and courage. [*Exit.*]

EDWARD.

So, we must ascend the Calvary that we may reach to glory. It has ever been so. This hitherto inscrutable decree of Providence has now been unravelled by the light of Spiritualism. How could we realize the joy awaiting us in the world to come,

without having first experienced its antithesis, pain? And just
as night was made to enable us to enjoy the light of day, and
the storm that we may admire the pure sky, so our sufferings
are the sure pledge of the bliss to come. O Heavenly Father!
in this, the greatest trial of my life, I fervently ask Thy sup-
port, and the power of saying, with a less sad heart, Thy will
be done!

SCENE III.

Rosaline and the Same.

Rosaline.

Good-morning, sir.

Edward.

Good-morning, Rosaline. What tidings do you bring me?
How is Miss Grasp?

Rosaline.

My dear young mistress bears up wonderfully under her great
sorrow. She wishes me to tell you that, by the desire of her
father, she is to accompany Mrs. Grasp to their country seat,
where most likely they will remain a long time. The departure
is fixed for to-morrow; and Miss Eleanor, wishing to take leave
of you, would be glad that you should see her this evening
in their garden. Here is the double key of the conservatory.
[*Handing him a key.*]

Edward.

I shall be there in an hour.

Rosaline.

I must also tell you that Master has given orders to the servants to intercept all letters to and from Miss Eleanor; therefore I am sent as her messenger.

Edward.

I feel much obliged for your kind errand.

ROSALINE.

Let me express to you my admiration for the manner in which you bear this great disappointment; for I well know how strong must be your grief.

EDWARD.

Rosaline, a Spiritualist yourself, you should not be surprised at my resignation. We all know that no holy aspiration can remain unfulfilled, and I am convinced that, if not here, Eleanor will be my partner in heaven.

ROSALINE.

Oh, how consoling is our belief!

EDWARD.

I understand that you are a great clairvoyante.

ROSALINE.

I have seen spirits from my earliest childhood.

EDWARD.

This is a truly splendid gift.

ROSALINE.

But it has its unpleasant side.

EDWARD.

How?

ROSALINE.

Because I often see dark spirits surrounding men who are thought just and good, whereas the low spirits that follow them show that they are great hypocrites.

EDWARD.

True; rudimental spirits are always the attendants on bad thoughts and feelings.

SCENE IV.

JAMES and the Same.

JAMES.

Mr. Patience.

EDWARD.

Show him in. [*To* ROSALINE.] Say that I shall not fail at the meeting. [ROSALINE *bows, and exit.*]

———

SCENE V.

PATIENCE and EDWARD.

EDWARD.

I am very glad to see you, Mr. Patience. In what can I be of service to you?

PATIENCE.

Well, sir, after forty-five years of faithful service, Mr. Grasp has summarily dismissed me this morning, and I come to ask the favor of your recommending me to another situation.

EDWARD.

Sent you away without notice! and what for?

PATIENCE.

Because, rather than oppress with law proceedings two of his poor debtors, I preferred paying their small debts from my own pocket.

EDWARD.

It seems ordained that we must suffer even for doing good. The new philosophy that has come to illumine the world teaches us that the trials of this life are sent to make us understand the blessings of the next. Meanwhile be of good cheer. I will speak to my uncle in the city, who might give you employment.

PATIENCE.

I feel much obliged to you. In speaking of a new philosophy, you were, no doubt, alluding to Spiritualism. My many occupations have hitherto prevented me from investigating these new theories, which, by having attracted the attention of your worthy father and of yourself, cannot but be deserving of inquiry.

EDWARD.

Spiritualism numbers amongst its ranks some of the most eminent men of Europe and America.

PATIENCE.

Although I am quite settled in my religious opinions, being a convinced Christian, yet I should like to know what are the points of divergence between the two doctrines.

EDWARD.

If you are a Christian, you are a Spiritualist, as we Spiritualists are Christians in the broadest sense of the word. Immortality of the soul, punishment or reward according to our deeds, communion of the saints, are doctrines common to both beliefs. If authorities were wanting to show that Spiritualism and Christianity agree, I might name Origenes, Tertullian, Whately, and other eminent ecclesiastics of ancient and modern times, all agreeing Spiritualism to be the very key to that grand yet mysterious book, the Christian Bible. The only difference that can be discerned between Christianity and Spiritualism is that we know what you believe, and you believe what we know, and to your *Memento mori* we reply *Memento vivere*.

PATIENCE.

In truth, one cannot deny the Bible to be anything else but a history of the Spiritualism of the past; but I should like to know something of the ethics of Spiritualism.

EDWARD.

The subject is too vast to be exhausted in a brief conversation, since Spiritualism is at the same time a science, a philosophy, and a religion: a science, because it is founded on ascertained facts; a philosophy, because it enters the vast domain of morals; and a religion, because it treats of the soul and its destiny. Spiritualism can indeed be defined the science of religion, the religion of science, and the philosophy of philosophies.

PATIENCE.

I should like to know something of the dialectics of Spiritualism.

EDWARD.

A very wide field indeed, of which I can give you but an imperfect outline. We learn, then, that all the worlds that stud the firmament are so many cradles and schools for infinite humanity; that these material worlds were made to develop the human body; that the material body was made to develop the human spirit; and that the human spirit, this individualized spark from the great central focus, is destined to everlasting progression. On casting aside the mortal coil, the spirit finds itself clothed with an ethereal body imperishable like the soul, and with which it can travel through space with the rapidity of thought. The eye becomes then the channel of speech, for thought is visible to the spirit. Reward and punishment are awarded according to our deeds in the earthly career. Remorse is the attendant on the transgressors of divine laws, and is not given as a punishment, but as a means of purification, that the spirit may, thus redeemed, return to Him that created it.

PATIENCE.

I can see here a marked difference between our respective creeds; for you do not seem to admit eternal punishment, or those localities, the heaven and hell of the Christians.

EDWARD.

Heaven and hell are not localities, but states, which we carry within us; and as for the eternity of sufferings, only unthinking theologians believe in such a paradoxical theory, forgetting what is said in Holy Writ, that "the wrath of God does not last for ever." The idea of an infinite punishment is not consistent with the mercy, the wisdom, or the prescience of God. We, the children of a loving Father, cannot but be destined to inherit his eternal love. A Greek word in the Bible being translated in the sense of *everlasting*, instead of its true meaning which is *long lasting*, has been the cause of that serious misapprehension.

PATIENCE.

A convocation of bishops is now engaged in revising the translation of the Bible. I understand that many of them are great scholars of the ancient Greek, and it is to be hoped that they will not overlook this important point, and correct the error.

EDWARD.

The sooner they do it the better for their credit and their conscience; for they ought to know that this frightful and revolting theory of eternal vengeance is the principal source of atheism in the world.

PATIENCE.

One more question: I am told that not unfrequently very unruly spirits take possession of your mediums and frighten the assistants at your seances. Is this so?

EDWARD.

It is quite true; and your question offers me the opportunity of calling your attention to what constitutes, perhaps, the most remarkable and interesting phase of modern Spiritualism. A number of these spirits which we call rudimental, believing in their ignorance that they are condemned forever, try to revenge themselves by doing all the evil in their power; but, treated by us with pity and kindness, and taught the infinite mercy of God and the law of progression, they are rendered docile, and by degrees made to enter the realms of light. I myself have been instrumental in enlightening hundreds of these unhappy souls. It is truly consoling to see the gratitude expressed by those converted spirits, first to God, and then to us His humble instruments. The discovery of this hitherto unknown power in mortals to benefit the inhabitants of the spirit-world is, you must admit, a truly wonderful fact.

PATIENCE.

Nothing more stupendous! I suppose many works are written on Spiritualism. Could you oblige me with the title of some of them, as you have awakened an interest in me to know more upon the subject.

6

EDWARD.

Thousands of volumes, in all languages, have been published on this new revelation. I possess a good number of them in our idiom, which I place at your disposal.

PATIENCE.

I shall profit by your kind offer. Let me now thank you for the instruction you have imparted to me, as well as for the interest you take in my behalf.

EDWARD.

I have only done my duty, and you may always look upon me as a friend.

PATIENCE.

I again thank you, and wish you good-bye.

EDWARD.

Good-bye, good-bye! [*Exit* PATIENCE.] [EDWARD *looking at his watch.*] The time for the fatal meeting is approaching, and I do not know whether I most wish or dread the interview which may, alas! be the last on earth with her whom I so deeply love. May Providence give me strength to bear this trial!

ACT VI.

SCENE I.

GRASP'S drawing-room. Night.

GRASP.

Mine has been a bold resolve. It was a choice of dangers, and I have preferred the least. Who can ever suspect *me* of murder? And if they did, my gold will save me. But the hour of the execution of my device has passed, and I cannot help feeling rather anxious.

SCENE II.

THOMAS and the Same.

THOMAS.

Please, sir, two very ill-looking individuals, who would neither give their names, nor tell their errand, insist upon seeing you. They look such ugly customers, that perhaps you would wish me to stand near the door of the parlor and come to your aid if necessary.

GRASP.

It is all right, Thomas; I know who they are. They belong to my warehouse. You stay here until my return. [*Exit.*]

THOMAS.

What nice warehousemen those are of Master's, to be sure! They look more like bulldogs than human beings. And why did Master wish me to stay here? With due respect for my superiors, I don't believe a word that those two brutes belong to the warehouse. They must be two cut-throats, and I smell here a very big rat, which will soon fall into the trap of my understanding.

SCENE III.

GRASP and the Same.

GRASP.

[*Somewhat out of breath.*] Thomas, you may return to the hall. [THOMAS *bows, and exit.*] It is done; and Complis at the bottom of the Thames cannot hurt me now. Instead of three thousand pounds, three hundred pieces of gold have freed me from that villain. But — oh, horrible thought! — that document may yet be found in the pocket of the drowned man! If so, my ruin is certain! The water may fortunately have obliterated the writing, and I must trust to my usual good luck.

SCENE IV.

COMPLIS and the Same.

COMPLIS.

Good evening, Mr. Grasp. How do you do?

GRASP.

[*Shrinking with horror, and to himself.*] Good heavens! What is this?

COMPLIS.

Why, Mr. Grasp, you seem frightened! Surely you have not become a Spiritualist, believing in the return of the dead! Behold me, Ernest Complis, in flesh and blood! So, so, — you have thrown away three hundred pounds, which you might have added to the paltry three thousand you wanted to stint me of!

GRASP.

What do you mean? I do not understand you.

COMPLIS.

I mean that the two boys you commissioned to shove me into the Thames happened to be my chums, and that you may now consider yourself a transported convict.

GRASP.

Don't speak so loud, you demon! I will keep my word; and if you have brought that accursed document, you shall have the three thousand pounds you extort from me.

COMPLIS.

You mistake the figure, Angel Grasp. The pounds must be five thousand this time.

GRASP.

You are mad! You want to ruin me!

COMPLIS.

To ruin you would require another Grasp.

GRASP.

Come, where is that paper?

COMPLIS.

The paper is here. [*Places the right hand in his breast-pocket, and draws a revolver, then a paper, which he shows to* GRASP.]

GRASP.

Wait, and I will fetch the three thousand pounds.

COMPLIS.

[*Pointing the revolver at him.*] I say five, man!

GRASP.

Perdition! [*Exit.*]

COMPLIS.

You shall not try your hand on me again, you desperate vagabond! [*Takes a small box from his pocket and places it under a couch.*] Before morning it will be said, "Here was the house of Merchant Grasp."

GRASP.

[*Returning with a roll of papers in his hands.*] Here is the money. Give me the paper.

COMPLIS.

I might ask to have the money handed first; but I have great confidence in your delicacy, Mr. Grasp. [*Hands the document to* GRASP.]

GRASP.

[*Takes the document, and, after scrutinizing it attentively, places the money on the table.*] Count your money.

COMPLIS.

It is soon done. — Five bank-notes of one thousand each, and all good. You have ever been an honorable man. Nothing remains for me to do now than to wish you a very good-night.

GRASP.

Recollect, Mr. Complis, that we are in each other's keeping yet.

COMPLIS.

That is, you rather more in mine than I in yours. Good-night, sir; good-night. [*Exit.*]

GRASP.

That man may destroy me yet. At any cost, I must try to make him disappear. [*Exit.*]

SCENE V.

GRASP'S garden. ELEANOR and ROSALINE.

ELEANOR.

You see, Rosaline, that there are positions in life when necessity overrules conventionality. It is not without much hesitation that I have convened Edward here; for were my parents to know of this meeting, it would grieve them. But I could not resist the wish of pressing for the last time that hand which I hoped to have been given to me at the altar in the temple.

ROSALINE.

Dear Mistress, I cannot see any harm in what you are doing. As for your fears of meeting Mr. Edward for the last time, let me remind you that as long as there is life there is hope. — But I hear steps. — I think I see him. — Here he comes, and I retire.

[*Exit.*]

SCENE VI.

EDWARD and ELEANOR.

EDWARD.

Sweet friend, thanks for granting me this interview.

ELEANOR.

Dear Edward, our meeting will be a sad one; for I fear, alas! it may be the last on earth, as the opposition of my parents to our union is irrevocable.

EDWARD.

I feared as much. All that remains to us now is resignation and submission to the Divine decrees. I always felt that to have you as a partner in life was a blessing fit only for angels. Let us wait, then, until we leave this world of strife, and be joined in the spheres of harmony.

ELEANOR.

Apart from you I shall not tarry long on this earth, my beloved. Grieve not when I am gone, for I shall ever be at your side awaiting to receive you when you are called.

EDWARD.

Our departure hence is ruled by the Highest Wisdom. Would it were written above that we might leave hand in hand this vale of tears, where all soon fades away.

ELEANOR.

And reach jointly that land of eternal bliss, where everything ever begins anew, and where love and all true aspirations of the soul are sure to be realized. And now, Edward, adieu.

EDWARD.

Adieu, Eleanor. May angels be with you!

ELEANOR.

[*Joining her hands, and looking upwards.*] Almighty Ruler of the universe, we thank Thee even for this bitter cup, as we are thankful for the knowledge Thou hast given us that all is for our ultimate good. Grant us to be resigned for the time allotted us here below, and then deign to receive us amongst the blessed. [*To* EDWARD.] Adieu, Edward; adieu.

EDWARD.

Adieu, Eleanor; adieu, dearest friend. May angels keep you company! [*They embrace; exit* EDWARD.]

ELEANOR.

[*Looking fondly after* EDWARD.] Yes, farewell! Farewell for ever in this world!

ROSALINE.

Dear Miss Eleanor, have more faith. Who knows that God may not make your parents relent?

ELEANOR.

To Him all is possible; but I have a strong conviction that Edward and I shall only meet next in heaven.

ROSALINE.

Where we shall be all happy together.

ELEANOR.

And where we shall call each other *sisters*. [*Exit both.*]

SCENE VII.

GRASP and THOMAS advancing cautiously, GRASP having
revolvers in his hands.

GRASP.

Are you sure you saw a man in this garden just now?

THOMAS.

Yes, sir, as distinctly as I see you now. I saw him enter from
the conservatory.

GRASP.

What was his appearance?

THOMAS.

He looked like a gentleman.

GRASP.

Might it have been that fellow, Complis?

THOMAS.

He was of the same height; but I can't be sure it was him.

GRASP.

Thomas, go and wake up the gardener; tell him to watch all
night, and shoot at any man he sees on these grounds. I shall
be responsible for the deed. Be also careful to secure the door
of the house leading to the garden, and bring me the key before
I go to bed. [*Exit.*]

THOMAS.

Mysteries increase and multiply in this house. I see a man
in the garden, and a moment afterwards he disappears, leaving
the gates all closed behind him. Master gets terribly alarmed,
suspecting the man to be Complis, and giving murderous orders
in consequence. What can all this mean? I never was so puz-
zled in my life, and I would give anything to find it all out. I
will obey orders, and wake up the gardener; and I hope to goodness that no one will be found dead here to-morrow.

SCENE VIII.

Drawing-room in Dr. New's house.

Dr. New.

I would my son were back. His meeting Eleanor in the garden of that man was a hazardous step, for I believe Grasp capable of any excess. Oh, the corrupting influence of gold! No one could have been more generous or kind-hearted than he was when a youth; but no sooner had he inherited a large fortune than the demons of avarice and ambition took possession of his soul. Examples like this, though of most frequent occurrence, seem to read no lesson to the parents of our times, who, instead of leaving to their children the treasures of a good education and of a well-formed heart, think only of accumulating wealth, which becomes a vest of Nessus for their luckless offspring. Ah, Spiritualism has not come too soon for the enlightenment of the present generation.

SCENE IX.

Edward and the Same.

Dr. New.

Edward, I am glad to see you back, for I was rather thoughtful about you. Have you seen and taken leave of that dear child?

Edward.

Yes, dear father.

Dr. New.

Has she shown firmness and resignation of heart at parting with you?

Edward.

Nothing could be more admirable than her behavior on so trying an occasion. She is truly one of God's elect, and very little removed from an angelic being.

DR. NEW.

How different from her parents! Although Spiritualism explains many a mystery in nature, yet it hides from us the reason of the great disparity of character often observed between parents and children.

EDWARD.

Unless indeed we look for an explanation of this fact in the reality of reincarnation, a doctrine to which we pay so little attention, and even spurn, in England, although admitted by some of the greatest minds in all ages.

DR. NEW.

Nothing more reprehensible than rejecting a theory without examining it. In their objection to look into this doctrine on the part of the majority of English and American Spiritualists, and condemning it *a priori*, they do not perceive that they only imitate the would-be men of science who act in the like manner in regard to Spiritualism.

EDWARD.

You are quite right, father. I mean to investigate the claims of the theory of reincarnation, which *prima facie* seems to me reasonable.

DR. NEW.

But it is now late; let us retire. Good night, Edward. Cheer up, my boy; and God bless you!

EDWARD.

Good night, dear father. [*Exit at opposite sides of the stage.*]

SCENE X.

JAMES.

Poor Master Edward, how sad he has been looking of late! It must be on account of the refusal he has received from Mr. Grasp, who thought perhaps that he was not good enough for his daughter. But he may go far and wide and never find such a son-in-law as my young master. Oh, these rich people are so unreasonable! They think that gold is happiness, as if they could carry that happiness into the next world! Ah, there are neither rich nor poor there; and as God is just, we hard-working people must fare better than they in the life to come. [*A clock sounding midnight is heard.*] Midnight is sounding, and I will go to bed. [*Cries of fire are heard from many voices in the street.*] What! fire? My goodness, wherever can it be? [*Goes to the window, throws it open, and a great glare of fire is seen.*] Good gracious! Mr. Grasp's house is in flames! I must awaken my masters!

SCENE XI.

DR. NEW and EDWARD rushing in.

JAMES.

Master! Mr. Grasp's house is on fire!

EDWARD.

[*Looking out of the window.*] Good heavens! it is so! Father, I go!

DR. NEW.

Go, my son! Would that my age allowed me to go with you! [*Exit EDWARD.*] [DR. NEW *looking out of the window.*] The fire seems a very serious one. Fortunately, here comes the fire brigade.

SCENE XII.

ROSALINE and the Same.

ROSALINE.

Doctor, what are we to do? We are lost! All the first floor of Master's house is in a blaze. Thomas and I attempted to rouse the family, but we found the stairs all on fire; and as Master had all the issues of the house locked and had possession of the keys, Thomas, I, and the other servants have escaped by the window.

DR. NEW.

There is still hope. I see the firemen approach the escape-ladder to the windows.

ROSALINE.

But I don't see them opened; and I am afraid the smoke has smothered all within! There, I see Mr. Edward and Thomas helping the firemen in all their operations! Heaven protect us! I see the flames issuing from the roof, and all hope for saving the family is over! [*A great crash is heard.*] Good God! the roof has fallen in, and the house is a heap of ruins!

DR. NEW.

What has become of my son? Can you see him?

ROSALINE.

I can see neither him nor Thomas. May God protect them!

JAMES.

There is Thomas; I see him coming this way!

ROSALINE.

Heaven be praised!

DR. NEW.

James, go and look for my son! Make haste! [*Exit* JAMES.]

ROSALINE.

[*Looking spellbound out of the window, as if in a trance.*] What do I see! O beautiful sight! My dear young Mistress rising from the ruins as a bright spirit, surrounded by an angel host, all shining with light! — And there! — there! — I see also the spirits of Master and Mistress striving to follow their daughter, but they cannot soar, and fall back to the ground! — Listen! Their daughter says to them, "Hope, dear mother! hope, dear father! I shall pray for you, and you shall come with me!"

DR. NEW.

Say, do you see my son?

ROSALINE.

Not in spirit.

DR. NEW.

God grant that he has been spared!

SCENE XIII.

THOMAS and PATIENCE, carrying COMPLIS wounded.

ROSALINE.

You are safe, Thomas! God be praised!

PATIENCE.

Doctor, here is one of the victims of the fire.

DR. NEW.

What! Mr. Complis?

THOMAS.

Yes, sir. He was watching the fire, when the fire-engine knocked him down, and hurt him badly.

DR. NEW.

How unfortunate! Place him here. [*Pointing to a couch. Exit* THOMAS *and* PATIENCE, *whilst the* DOCTOR *and* ROSALINE *place themselves near the couch.*] [*Feeling the pulse of* COMPLIS.] Mr. Complis! Mr. Complis!

COMPLIS.

[*Very faintly.*] It is all over with me, Doctor! Before it be too late, I will confess that it is I who am the incendiary of that house!

ROSALINE.

Oh, horrible deed!

DR. NEW.

Can that be? And why did you do that?

COMPLIS.

Fear and revenge led me to it. May God have mercy upon me! [*Falls back and dies.*]

DR. NEW.

It is all over; life is extinct.

SCENE XIV.

PATIENCE, THOMAS, and the Same. PATIENCE and THOMAS carrying the senseless body of EDWARD NEW, which they place on another couch.

PATIENCE.

Dr. New, here is your son, much hurt, I fear.

DR. NEW.

Oh, Edward! Oh, my dear child! [*Rushes towards the motionless body of* EDWARD, *and feels his pulse.*] He breathes still! but I have, alas! no hope of saving him!

THOMAS.

Don't say that, Doctor! It is dreadful to think that he should die so young!

DR. NEW.

There is no death, my friend. What we call death is only a step into eternity.

ROSALINE.

Oh, save him, Doctor, if you can! He is so good!

DR. NEW.

It is too late! My son is now with the angels!

[*They all gather around the couch of* EDWARD, *and immediately from the back of it three spirits are seen to rise, being those of the* DOCTOR'S WIFE, *of* EDWARD, *and of* ELEANOR; *the latter hand in hand, and the former a little higher, in the act of blessing them.*]

ROSALINE.

[*Pointing to the spirits.*] I see them! I see them! There, there! How beautiful!

DR. NEW.

What do you see?

ROSALINE.

Your son and my angel young mistress rising together, and your sainted wife blessing them!

DR. NEW.

Oh, would that I had the divine gift of spiritual sight! — Hail, my dear wife! I bless you, my son! I bless you, my daughter! I shall soon be with you!

[*At this moment, from behind the couch where the body of* COMPLIS *is lying, his spirit is seen to rise, dressed in a dark-gray long robe, his face partly covered, and in an attitude of distress and repentance.*]

ROSALINE.

[*Turning her eyes towards the new apparition.*] Ha!

N. B. Should the drama be represented on the stage, it is well to observe that the body of EDWARD NEW, brought in dying, must not be the real one but a substitute, as he must appear in the apotheosis. Not so with COMPLIS, whose spirit may be represented by another person, taking the precaution of hiding the face of the apparition. In order to imitate as well as possible a spirit-apparition, it would be well to show it reflected in a so-called *optical mirror*, such as was used by Professor Pepper at the Polytechnic Institution in London to show how a spectre could appear. The three spirits of the first tableau should all be dressed in white, — ELEANOR as a bride, with veil and wreath, and EDWARD as a genius.

www.ingramcontent.com/pod-product-compliance
Lightning Source LLC
Chambersburg PA
CBHW020028030726
47499CB00007B/2320